# Beautifully Broken

## Emory

Copyright © 2019 by Emory
All rights reserved.

No part of this book may be reproduced or transmitted in any form or by any means, electronic or mechanical, including photocopying, recording, or by any information storage and retrieval system without the written permission of the author, except for the use of brief quotations in a book review.

This book is a work of fiction. Names, characters, places, and incidents either are products of the author's imagination or are used fictitiously. Any resemblance to actual persons, living or dead, events, or locales is entirely coincidental.

ISBN: 9781074640637

*Emmy*

Thank you for your support Krista!

# CONTENTS

    Book Playlist

| | | |
|---|---|---|
| 1 | Chapter One | Pg 1 |
| 2 | Chapter Two | Pg 13 |
| 3 | Chapter Three | Pg 30 |
| 4 | Chapter Four | Pg 42 |
| 5 | Chapter Five | Pg 68 |
| 6 | Chapter Six | Pg 93 |
| 7 | Chapter Seven | Pg 118 |
| 8 | Chapter Eight | Pg 131 |
| 9 | Chapter Nine | Pg 151 |
| 10 | Chapter Ten | Pg 164 |
| 11 | Chapter Eleven | Pg 195 |
| 12 | Chapter Twelve | Pg 217 |
| | Acknowledgements | Pg 225 |
| | About the Author: Emory | Pg 229 |

# Book Playlist

1. Hallelujah by Tori Kelly
2. Irregular Heartbeat by 50 Cent
3. Demons by Jasmine Thompson (cover version)
4. Shallow by Lady Gaga and Bradley Cooper
5. Out Queens by Prodigy
6. I'm a Mess by Bebe Rexha
7. Get Dealt With by Mobb Deep
8. Affirmative Action by Nas
9. Un-thinkable by Alicia Keys
10. Out of Love by Alessia Cara
11. Drop a Gem On Em by Mobb Deep
12. High All the Time by 50 Cent
13. I love you by Billie Eilish
14. G'D Up by G-Unit
15. N.Y. State of Mind by Nas
16. Only Hope by Mandy Moore
17. Scars to Your Beautiful by Alessia Cara
18. La La La by Jasmine Thompson (cover version)
19. Who You Are by Jessie J
20. Shutter Island by Jessie Reyez

# Chapter One

While the sun and moon trade places in the sky, steamy Brooklyn streets come alive with distant police sirens and the usual hustle and bustle of commuters. Jaxon rounds the corner, entering a graffitied back alley. He spots his friend Elijah taking bets while two fighters prepare to do battle.

"What's up Jaxon, you aren't fighting tonight?" Elijah counts the money, giving Jaxon a fist bump.

"Nah man, I'm just spectating tonight. I'll get in on the bet though. What's the story on these two?" Jaxon leans his back against the wall, adjusts his beanie, and rubs his hand across his stubbled face.

Elijah grins, looking at Jaxon over the top of his glasses "Alright, the big Viking looking dude, that's Erickson. Just got out of prison a month ago, and this dude is as mean as they come. I heard he punched a guy so hard he went into a coma. Sounds a little farfetched to me, but hey what do I know, I'm just here to count the money".

"Sounds like I need to fight this guy in my next bout" Jaxon shuffles loose gravel under his shoes.

Elijah wears a contempt expression "Now is this coming from Jaxon, the up-and-coming fighter or the Jaxon who's still beating himself up over his brother's death?".

Jaxon shrugs, jamming his hands into his front pockets "I'm just saying, he'd still be alive if I hadn't caused a scene that night. You know I'm right".

Elijah claps Jaxon's shoulder "And he may not be. He made a decision, just like you did. It's time you accept that and quit punishing yourself bro. Purposely taking hits from these guys like you do, just because you feel guilty, it's only going to be so long before you can't get up anymore".

Jaxon ignores Elijah's sentiment, focusing his attention back to the fight "I got a hundred on Erickson".

Jaxon hands Elijah a hundred-dollar bill and gets lost in his thoughts "I'm going to make this right Harvey, for you brother. Right now though, I gotta do this my way. I know, I know, alcohol and fighting are the reasons you're looking at me from above, but hey you're my guardian angel now. Don't let me down like I did you. I love you brother".

Jaxon's thoughts are interrupted by Elijah going over the rules for the fight "Alright! Let's get one thing clear, this isn't some little underground fight club. This is "Knuckle Up" fight ring. We fight above ground, wherever we want. We aren't afraid of a little publicity! Fighters! You can spill into the streets or you can keep it back here in the alley. But if you're going to take it to the streets, make sure you give the citizens of Brooklyn a good show!".

The crowd cheers.

Elijah continues "The fight goes until one fighter can't get up, gets knocked out cold, or gives up. We got the usual lookouts for New York's finest so be ready for a good old-fashioned foot chase if it comes to that. As always, two grand goes to the winner. So, let's get this show on the road already! Fighters, KNUCKLE UP!"

Just a couple minutes in and Erickson's fists bounce the opponent's face off the concrete, blood dripping rapidly from the fighter's mouth. Jaxon makes a jerking glance at a side door being swung open next to him. A trash bag heaved from inside makes its' way into the steel dumpster.

His forehead creases "Man come on, shut the door at least".

Jaxon makes his way over, peering around the corner.

"Hmm, no one there." He says under his breath.

Jaxon turns his face back towards the fight, but not for long. His ear drums are surrounded by a woman's sweet husky voice singing inside the concert hall.

Goosebumps cover his skin as she sings a familiar song "It doesn't matter what you heard, the holy or the broken, hallelujah".

Jaxon spaces out, her voice enchants him like a siren would a sailor, "Hallelujah, Hallelujah, Hallelujah, Hallelujah".

He follows her voice down the hall, approaching a room full of faces transformed in awe. He sneaks in, looking towards the stage.

His face lights up "Wow, she is stunning. Her white dress, the way her long curly blonde hair falls over her shoulders. She looks like an angel… And sounds like one too".

Jaxon makes his way to the back of the room, sits at the bar, and watches her sing.

     A standing ovation brings a dimpled smile to the girls face and an end to her set. She makes the trek backstage, giving a final wave to the cheering crowd.

"Paisley, you killed it out there! The crowd loved you. I even heard some cute guys asking about you" her friend runs up with outstretched arms.

"Thanks, Londyn" Paisley forces a half smile, taking a seat on a padded bench.

Londyn grabs a metal folding chair and sits next to Paisley.

She takes Paisley's hand in hers and softens her

tone "Hey… I didn't forget today marks two years since his death. I was just hoping to cheer you up".

Paisley draws in a long breath "I'm sorry Londyn. I know, I should be more excited. It's my first big show and I didn't totally choke out there, but I guess a piece of me feels selfish for wanting to be happy".

Londyn cuts in, encouragement in her voice "You're allowed to be happy. Heck, you're even allowed to date again. Girl, you're a catch! I mean, it's been two years and you haven't even had a single date. And talking to customers at work does not constitute a date!".

"Hey, I enjoy what I do" Paisley jabs playfully, wrapping a curl around her finger.

"Ugh, I don't know how you do it. I could never be a waitress. Smiling at people. Waiting on their every need. Pretending to be interested in their dry conversations all night. Sounds like a bad dream to me" Londyn shudders.

Paisley rolls her eyes, giggling "Don't even play, you're more outgoing than I am".

"And you're nicer than I am" Londyn's eyebrows raise.

"I guess that's why everyone says you're the fire to my ice. Which I kind of never really got because wouldn't ice mean I'm like, cold-hearted or something?" Paisley ponders, drawing the corner of her lower lip between her teeth.

"Girl… you're thinking too much into it" Londyn shakes her head "pretty sure they just mean I'm a bitch".

"Maybe. You kind of are" Paisley smirks, bracing for a playful punch from Londyn.

A fun-loving sarcastic smile crosses Londyn's face "Ha ha. Let's just go eat already, before you change your mind".

The friends exit the building and begin their short walk to a late-night café.

Paisley turns to Londyn "Ok, serious question. Do you ever feel like someone is watching you?".

"What do you mean?" Londyn raises a brow, her eyes fill with curiosity.

"I don't know, like, lately I've had this eerie feeling that I'm being watched. Like someone bad is waiting for the right time to make a move. I'll be in my apartment, minding my own business when suddenly my skin starts to crawl, and my anxiety takes over. The walls start closing in and I feel like I'm going to pass out. Even when I'm at the store. The other day, I got so paranoid, I just walked right out and left a cart full of groceries behind because I couldn't take it" Paisley cringes.

"Paisley, you're as sweet as pie. I don't know anyone that would want to hurt you, let alone wish any ill will your way. Look, I'm sure it's just in your head. This time of the year is hard for you and I get it. I mean, what you saw was tragic. Anyone would have been wrecked. And, I wish they would have caught the guy, but the police did reassure it was a random incident. Some creep in the park seized an opportunity" Londyn reassures, opening the door to the café.

"You're probably right" Paisley sighs.

Londyn pats Paisley's shoulder, comforting her "I hate it too. Just… don't let him run around in your head too long. He doesn't deserve a spot there. Now come on, let's get you a strong espresso".

The next day, Paisley's crowded tables keep her on her toes. Her fifteen-minute break to recharge comes not a moment too soon. She takes a seat at an empty table and pulls out her phone to read a text from Londyn.

"Hey girl, lets go dancing tonight. I'm bringing Ted and he's bringing his friend, Brent. Don't worry, it's not a date. Do you think you'll be off in time?".

Paisley sets her phone down and sighs, rubbing her temples.

"I would literally rather do anything else. Dancing, crowds, people. Whatever happened to popcorn and a movie cuddled up on the couch... Oh my gosh, am I twenty-one or forty-one" she thinks, laying her head down, pretending to bang it on the table.

"Are you ok Paisley?" her coworker Macie approaches.

"Oh, Macie, hey. Yeah, I'm fine, just thinking" Paisley chews at a fingernail.

Macie wears a puzzled expression "Ooookay. Umm, I was going to see if you'd be able to close for me tonight. I".

"Yes!" Paisley answers hurriedly before Macie finishes asking, knowing she would have the perfect excuse for not being able to go out.

"Are you sure? I mean, I could ask Gina instead if you need some time off. I feel like you're always here" Macie takes a sympathetic tone.

"I'm sure Macie, trust me" Paisley smiles politely.

"Ok. Thank you so much, you're the best!" a giddy Macie bends over and wraps Paisley in a hug.

"Oh, and Paisley" Macie sets her palms down flat on the table.

Paisley wears a curious expression, looking up at Macie.

"If you ever need anything… someone to talk to. I'm here. You know that right?" Macie fiddles with her bracelet.

"Yeah… Of course, thank you Macie" Paisley fidgets uncomfortably as Macie walks away.

Paisley focuses back on her phone and begins a text to Londyn "Sorry, I told Macie I would close for her tonight. I won't be off in time to get ready. You guys have fun though ok? And be safe".

Paisley slumps back into the booth, getting lost in a flashback.

*"Honey, we've got to get out more often. Let's go for dinner and a walk in the park under the stars tonight" William's voice sincere.*

*Paisley's heart skips a beat as William bends to one knee in the middle of the park.*

*"Paisley... will you marry me?" William smiles from ear to ear.*

*"Oh my gosh! Yes!" Paisley exclaims, wrapping William in a hug.*

*Her smile fades as William is ripped from her grasp.*

*"We don't want any trouble" William puts his hands up in surrendering fashion.*

*He tries to wrestle the knife from the man wearing a full-face ski mask with a Glasgow smile stitched into it.*

*"Run Paisley!" he yells.*

*Paisley watches in horror as the knife enters William's stomach, the life leaving his eyes while he falls face down on the pavement.*

She takes a sharp breath and snaps out of it.

Paisley breathes shakily, feeling anxious. But what she doesn't feel, is the pair of eyes watching her through the window from across the street. A minute passes before she stands to her feet, shoves her curly hair back away from her face, and composes herself.

"Why don't you smile anymore?" The man grumbles under his breath, watching Paisley get back to work, "It has been two years and you still can't stomach an emotion when we pass. Every single time, my smile is met by unknowing eyes. I should kill you Paisley. You ungrateful bit" he stops short of cursing her, wrapping his hands around the light pole as if strangling it "I'm sorry, I love you Paisley. Why can't you see the care in my eyes? Why don't I stand out to you? You should DIE! I should etch a permanent smile on your face, Paisley! But, I won't. What kind of man would I be if I hurt the woman I love? Someday my beauty, someday your eyes will light up when you see me".

## Chapter Two

Kent Gardens. Home to dimly lit, paint chipped stairwells, dirty elevators that seem ready to give out at any moment, air conditioners that hardly live up to their name, and... Jaxon. His nostrils take in the familiar smell of stale beer and lingering cigarette smoke as he steps inside and takes a final swig of his pint of whiskey. The empty bottle clangs off the inside of the trash can. He puffs his cheeks and breathes out, approaching the elevator.

"Usually, I feel good after a knockout victory. But right now, I just feel like shit. I don't know what it is" he thinks, stepping inside the elevator.

The elevator groans, slowly making its way to the sixth floor before the doors give their best effort at opening smoothly. Jaxon notices his sister, Morgan, standing next to his apartment door holding her sleeping daughter, Freya.

"Hey sis… Umm, it's nine o'clock at night. Is everything alright?" Jaxon approaches her with a hug and unlocks the door.

The siblings step inside. Jaxon sets his keys, wallet, and two thousand dollars on the counter while Morgan lays Freya down on the couch.

The floor creaks beneath Morgan's feet as she rounds the couch back to the cluttered kitchen counter "Elijah texted me a little bit ago. He's concerned about you. He said after you won your fight today, you just disappeared. I guess you vanished on him yesterday too. So, I thought Freya and I would pay you a visit and see how you're doing. Freya fell asleep in the car, but she's excited to tell you all about her gymnastics class".

Pouring two whiskeys and handing one to Morgan, a corner of Jaxon's mouth lifts "She's pretty talented. I can't wait to hear all about it. You guys haven't been waiting long have you? You know, you could've just come tomorrow".

Morgan takes the glass in her hand "We weren't waiting long, although if you'd make an extra key like I've suggested only a million times, we could have just let ourselves in instead of killing time in your creepy hallway" she teases.

Jaxon shrugs with a grin.

He tips his glass back, letting the whiskey quench his thirst before getting back on topic "You don't have to worry about me sis. I'll be alright, honestly, I will. You know Elijah, he tends to exaggerate things. Plus, I told him why I disappeared yesterday".

"Yeah, some pretty girl lured you away with her voice. He didn't buy it. I believe you though, you little hopeless romantic you" she nudges her brothers' shoulder.

"I'm twenty-two years old and you still make me feel fifteen" Jaxon chuckles, continuing "but for real, this girl, you should've seen her. She was like the type of girl you want to get down on one knee for and ask if you can change her last name".

"Dang Jaxon, she has you hearing wedding bells already?" Morgan's mouth curves into a mischievous smile.

"No, I'm just saying she LOOKS like that type of girl. I'm nowhere near ready for something like that. She was just… wholesome. But, a dangerously beautiful girl isn't going to make me go searching for her like she's the one that got away or something" Jaxon defends.

Morgan wears an unconvinced look on her face "who are you trying to convince, me or you?".

Jaxon face palms and pours more whiskey "never mind sis".

Morgan sets her glass down "But seriously Jaxon. This thing with Harvey, it sucks. It hit me hard too. I just don't want to see you spiral downward again, you know?".

"I've got it under control" Jaxon contends flimsily.

"Getting beat up on purpose and drinking alcohol like it's water is hardly in control. That fighting club, or whatever you call it, is trouble. I don't approve of it, mom wouldn't either, and dad would join just to kick your ass and tell you to get out of it. But let's face it, you're going to do what you want to do. If you set out for anyone's approval, you'd have a white picket fence, wife, and three kids".

"At twenty-two?" soft sarcasm enters Jaxon's voice.

Morgan rolls her eyes "You know what I mean. Just... promise me you'll be more careful".

Jaxon nods in agreement "It won't be like it was before, you have my word".

"I hope not. You spiraled after the shooting. You spiraled after Caroline. And, to be honest, it kind of looks like you're spiraling now. Don't get me wrong, you have a right to be angry. We both do. Just don't let the anger take control".

"Uncle Jaxon!" Freya jolts awake, jumps off the couch, and runs towards him with flailing arms.

"Hi sweet pea! I heard someone did great in gymnastics class. Any idea who that could be?" Jaxon picks his niece up, wrapping her in a hug.

Freya answers excitedly "ME!! Do you want to see what we did today!?".

"Of course! Let's see it" Jaxon lowers himself to her level.

Forty-five minutes of playing and

gymnastics routines later, Jaxon walks his sister and niece to their car and waves farewell as they pull away.

He leans his shoulder against a light pole, watching Morgan's taillights blend with the traffic.

"Sorry sis" he mumbles under his breath, reaching for a pint of bourbon housed within his inner jacket pocket.

"No, no, no! Ugh!" A woman's defeated tone grabs Jaxon's attention.

He turns around and watches the woman sulkily lean back against her car, pressing her hands to her cheeks.

He tucks the bourbon back in his pocket and starts in her direction "Hey... are you alright?"

The woman takes in a sharp breath and steps back, wishing she'd packed the pepper spray her friend bought her last Christmas.

"I'm sorry, I didn't mean to startle you" Jaxon lifts his hands, "I just live right here. It sounded like you needed some help".

As he draws closer, recognition dawns on his face.

"She's the gorgeous girl from the concert hall yesterday" he thinks, trying not to make it obvious he recognizes her.

Paisley gives him a once-over, living on a prayer "I'm sorry. I just get so jumpy this time of year".

"You're alright. Strange guy approaching at night in this area of town, it's understandable. I didn't mean to barge in on… whatever you've got going on" Jaxon rakes his fingers through his textured quiff hair.

Paisley looks through the passenger window "It's ok. The only thing you barged in on is the prolonged ending to my dreary day. Like an airhead, I locked my keys in my car".

"Ah, I see. Well, you may have caught a much-needed break then. I've got a sister who's locked her keys in her car more times than I can count. So much so, that I put together a lock pick set I keep in my car. I don't mind going to grab it really quick" Jaxon flashes a reassuring smile.

A sense of cautious relief overtakes Paisley "Are you sure? I'd hate to interrupt your night. And it's already so late".

Jaxon gives a dismissive wave "Trust me, I'm sure. It's just me and a cheap bottle of whiskey upstairs. Nothing important".

While Jaxon walks towards his car, Paisley looks heavenward "thank you" she thinks accompanied by a relieving sigh.

"Thank you so much for doing this, I really appreciate it" Paisley expresses her gratitude as Jaxon returns and begins to work on unlocking her car.

"You're welcome" Jaxon smiles.

An awkwardly silent minute passes before he tries his hand at small talk "so, um, if you don't mind me asking. Do you live around here?".

Paisley tucks a curl behind her ear "yeah, I actually live at Kent Gardens too. I'm 4A".

"I'm 6F. Nice place to live right?" Jaxon's tone facetious.

Paisley chuckles, playing along "yeah, comes with a whole laundry list of maintenance issues".

Jaxon grins, continuing to work on unlocking the car door "I'm surprised I haven't noticed you around here before".

"Why is that surprising?" Paisley's curiosity peaks.

"I don't know... You seem like someone worth remembering" Jaxon stammers, realizing he's getting ahead of himself as she's still unaware he saw her show the night before.

He squeezes his eyes shut and thinks "someone worth remembering? Wow, way to make it awkward Jax. Why don't you just confess your undying love right now".

"Oh... thank you" Paisley's voice softens as she unsuccessfully hides a smile.

It wasn't the most graceful compliment but hearing someone she doesn't even know say something so nice, it gave her heart a peaceful flutter.

"Alright, well, you're good to go" Jaxon steps away from the car as the lock is no longer doing its job.

"Thank you so much! You're a lifesaver" Paisley retrieves her keys, clutching them tight against her chest.

His heart warms "You're welcome, I'm glad I was able to help you out".

Jaxon opens the apartment complex door as he and Paisley step inside, making their way towards the overworked elevator.

"I swear, I feel like every time I ride this thing it's going to be my last" Jaxon teases as they step on.

Paisley giggles "Yeah. My best friend made me promise to tell her every time I get on here. She says, that way if she doesn't hear from me in a couple hours, she knows where to find me".

The elevator comes to a stop at Paisley's floor.

"So, um... I'll see you around?" Jaxon swims in her deep emerald eyes.

"Yeah... see you around" Paisley raises her hand in farewell, stepping off the elevator.

Paisley gets settled into her apartment, drawing a warm, candlelit bubble bath to wind down and relax after her exhausting day. She dangles her arm off the side of the tub and crosses her ankles in front of her. She takes in a deep breath, sighs, and closes her eyes.

"What a day" she thinks.

Paisley is transported into a dream as she dozes off.

*"A bath ten minutes before our reservation? Honey, we're going to be late" William stands in the doorway, shaking his head light heartedly.*

*Paisley tilts her head and flashes a pearly white smile "what if we just stayed in tonight?"*

*William's face goes blank.*

*"Sweetie?" Paisley looks on, confused as William stands silently at attention.*

*She covers her mouth with her hand as William's shirt soaks red. He falls towards her. A ski masked man with a stitched in Glasgow smile stands behind him, waving at her.*

"Oh my gosh!" Paisley startles awake, splashing bubbly water over the side of the tub.

Her chest rises and falls with rapid, anxious breaths. She moves her hair away from her face, looking nervously at the doorway.

She grabs her phone off the edge of the tub and sends a text to Londyn "Hey, are you still out?".

"No, Ted bailed, so I stayed home. What's up?" Londyn quickly texts back.

Paisley begins a call to her best friend and places her phone on speaker.

"Hey girl, are you alright?" Londyn answers, taking a sidesaddle position on her living room couch.

"Yeah, I'm just taking a bubble bath" Paisley plays off her ominous feeling.

"So, you're taking a relaxing bubble bath and decided to call the least relaxed person you know just to talk? What's really going on?" Londyn's voice straightforward.

Paisley gives up the façade "Sometimes I really hate that you can see right through me".

"It's a gift" Londyn smiles matter-of-factly.

Paisley picks at her nails "I dozed off a minute ago and had this creepy dream. Could you just talk to me for a bit, so I could feel less alone right now?".

Londyn grabs a piece of popcorn and pops it into her mouth "Of course. Do you want to tell me about your dream?".

Paisley side-eyes the doorway "No, but you'll never guess how my night ended".

"Uh oh, what happened? Londyn's eyes widen.

"As soon as I got home from work, I locked my

keys in my car. Thank goodness a guy who lives at my complex was outside and able to help. If not for him, I would probably still be out there waiting for a locksmith" Paisley leans the back of her head against the bathroom wall.

Londyn grins exuberantly "And was this guy cute?".

"Yeah" Paisley responds nonchalantly.

"Just yeah? Come on. I need more to go off of than just yeah" Londyn pushes playfully.

Paisley shrugs "I don't know... he was a good-looking guy. I guess he looked like the kind of guy who would get your number at the club and then never call you".

Londyn's interest peaks "In other words, I need to come over and lock my keys in my car too".

"You're so bad!" Paisley scoffs.

"Does this mystery guy have a name?" Londyn's voice eager.

Paisley scrunches up her face as she realizes she never got his name "Ummm...".

"Paisley! You didn't get his name!?" Londyn smacks her forehead.

"I mean… I just… My mind was occupied on not having my keys. I didn't even think to ask him" Paisley's face turns an embarrassed scarlet, "Can I earn some points back if I at least admit he did have a certain charm about him?".

Londyn plasters an accomplished smile on her face "You know what, you can. I'm not even going to push it. I'm just happy to hear you say that".

Two floors up, down a crooked hallway, Jaxon sits at his dining table, peering out the window. He holds an empty glass in one hand, a half-empty bottle of whiskey in the other. His eyes half open and glazed over, Jaxon drunkenly over pours. A puddle of whiskey drips from the table to the floor.

"Whatever" Jaxon slurs to himself, laying his arm in the whiskey puddle and his head on his bicep.

The shrill rings of his cell phone aren't enough to wake him from a drunken slumber.

On the other end of the phone, Elijah leaves a message "Hey Jax, I know you and Bishop still have heat between you. But he's a detective now and I called in a favor. It may be hard to believe, but he's doing this for you man, not me. Think about that before you see him. Anyways, he looked at your brother's case and found a connection to a murder a couple years ago. He wants to meet tomorrow morning. 8 o'clock at the 41st Street Café. Look, just give him a chance, that's all I'm asking. Call me back when you get this. I hope we'll see you there. Later man".

Paisley listens to the groaning sound of water draining from her bathtub, the lavender scented bubbles follow closely behind, still providing a comforting aroma "I can't believe I didn't get his name" she smiles, poking fun at herself.

"What was that?" Paisley quickly reaches for her towel, casting her eyes from side to side.

She makes herself still, trying not to breathe as if it would help her to listen closer.

"Is someone there?" Her voice quavers.

Paisley hears the rattle again, this time a click of

a lock follows.

"Shit!" she hurriedly wraps her towel around her body and turns off her bathroom light.

She presses her back against the wall, frantically looking for anything in her bathroom that could be used as a weapon. She settles on the broken towel rack she hasn't tried fixing yet.

"Did someone come inside? Should I look?" She contemplates, taking a deep breath "Ok, here goes nothing".

She sneaks her head around the corner, her eyes watching closely for any movement. She squints, trying to see if her door has been unlocked.

"Damnit, I can't tell" she moves from behind the bathroom wall, tiptoeing towards her front door.

She jerks a paranoid glance behind her and back towards the door where a shadow appears to be moving back and forth in the hallway.

She closes her eyes in frustration "of course I left my phone in the bathroom. I'm not going back now".

Paisley approaches the peep hole, relieved the door is still locked but nervous about who she may see behind it. And even more nervous whoever is there may see her. She's never trusted that peep holes are solely for one party to see while the other party stands there, unknowingly being judged.

She places her eye to the hole "No one there" she says, not trusting those words for a second.

She jumps back as her neighbor's door swings open, a woman leaving in a fit of rage "Fuck you Ronnie!".

"Sadie, baby, come on! Don't go" Ronnie half-heartedly tries but gives up as the door to the stairwell slams shut "whatever! You'll love me in the morning!".

Paisley giggles, comedically relieved. Ronnie closes his door, Paisley creaks hers open and looks down the empty hallway. She assumes a flickering light doing its best to keep the area lit was the shadowy culprit moving outside her door. As she shuts her door, she leans back against it, sliding down to a seated position.

She shakes her head "Either my paranoia has me hearing things or Ronnie and Sadie were louder than normal tonight... at least that's what I want to believe" she thinks.

## Chapter Three

The morning sun beams through Jaxon's curtainless windows, warming his eyelids. He opens his tired, bloodshot eyes, still gripping the full glass of whiskey he poured before passing out at his dining table last night. Jaxon yawns, rubbing his face to wake himself up.

He grabs his phone to check the time "Damn, it's only half passed seven... A missed call? I wonder what this is about" his tired voice mumbles, pushing play on Elijah's voice message.

Jaxon grits his teeth, as the very mention of his former best friend Bishop's name leaves a sour taste in his mouth. His stomach knots at the thought of seeing Bishop and having to hold back from laying a fist into his glass jaw. But he'd be lying if he said he wasn't curious about the connection to Harvey's murder. So, he makes a vow to himself. He will play nice… for now.

Jaxon tosses back his full glass of whiskey "breakfast of champions" he mutters aloud, pushing his chair out and away from the dining table to hurry and get ready for the meeting with Elijah and Bishop.

Jaxon runs his fingers through his hair, stumbling tiredly over an empty pizza box on the way to the bathroom. He removes his shirt and narrows his eyes at a set of faint gunshot scars near his abs and on his shoulder. Although the evidence shows it's been some time since he suffered the wounds, Jaxon won't ever forget the feeling of betrayal. It hurt worse than any bullet ever could.

    Jaxon approaches the 41st Street Café and spots Elijah and Bishop seated outside.

"Better late than never I guess" Elijah pushes his glasses back against his face, a sarcastic grin emerging.

"My bad bro, I had to check my surroundings

before I got here, make sure Bishop wasn't setting me up to get shot again" Jaxon glowers at Bishop.

Bishop folds his hands on the table "Nice to see you too Jaxon. I see it's always five o'clock somewhere for you ain't it? I can smell the whiskey way over here".

Elijah cuts in "alright guys, you got your jabs in. Are you happy? Now let's just get this over with".

Bishop shakes his head in annoyance "Alright. So, anyways, I'm here because Elijah asked me to look into Harvey's murder and see if I could find anything the investigators missed. And I may have. While I was looking, I got struck by deja vu when I realized the gash on his face resembled that of another victim two years ago in a murder at Flynn Park. This dude had apparently just proposed to his girlfriend. They were engaged for all of about thirty seconds before he was murdered right in front of her. It's the one case I haven't been able to shake. The brutality for no apparent reason. Our failure to give this woman closure by finding her fiancé's killer" Bishop leans in closer, "If he's surfaced, I've got a chance here to bring closure, not only to this woman but to you, Jaxon. The only thing is, I've got nothing on this guy. No fingerprints, no surveillance footage with his face, nothing".

Jaxon stands up to leave "So you're chasing a ghost. And you want us to, what, help you find your ghost? Don't take this the wrong way but I've got enough of my own problems. I don't need to take on yours too".

"The Jaxon I knew would've been all over this" Bishop slumps back against the metal chair.

Jaxon pounds his fist on the table, drawing gasps and attention from nearby patrons "The Jaxon you knew was left to die in a puddle of blood on the basketball court! You knew the hit on Miles was coming. You knew we played ball with him every Thursday at the park. But you sat back in that cushy squad car waiting for your opportunity to grab the bad guy. Well your timing sucked because when the shots rang out, who got hit three times? I did! Not Miles, me! You know who wouldn't have got hit if my homie would have tipped me off and, I don't know, told me not to show up to play ball that night? Me! So, excuse me if I'm not ready to jump all over your plan".

Bishop pushes his chair out, standing face to face with his former best friend "Look, I'm sorry Jaxon! I was a wide-eyed rookie who hung on every word his veteran superior had to say. How was I supposed to know he had his own agenda? You're right, I should've tipped you off and I failed you. Why do you think I'm here, offering you an olive branch? You think I didn't have nightmares about it too? If I could take it back, I would. But I can't. It's time we moved passed this. There's a killer out there and all I've got to go on is a description of the mask he wore two years ago. My position only allows me to get so far before people clam up. But someone out there knows something".

Jaxon clenches his fists, eyeing Bishop. One punch, that's all he'd like to deliver. Just one punch to Bishop's face.

Jaxon closes his eyes and takes a deep breath, composing himself "Alright Bishop. You want a fresh start? Fine. For Harvey and whoever this girl is, I'll help you find your ghost. But if you stab me in the back again, your murderer will be the least of your problems. Don't mistake this gesture for friendship either. If we're going to do this, we do it our way. Your police protocols and all that bullshit, we ain't got time for that".

Bishop gives an acknowledging nod. He and Jaxon share a tense handshake before returning to their seats.

Elijah breaks the silence "Bishop, you mentioned a mask? Why's that significant?".

Bishop takes a sip of water "Honestly, I'm not even sure it is. The fiancé was so traumatized by the experience, rightfully of course. But she mentioned he was wearing a ski mask with a Glasgow smile stitched into it. Most of us figured she conjured up that image because of the gash her fiancé was given from his cheek bone to his lip. You know, displace it to the killer's mask, make it easier to deal with".

Jaxon scoffs "Easier to deal with? Really? So, she displaces the image of her fiancé's gashed face to the killer's mask because she needed an easier way to deal with him being murdered right before her eyes? Do you hear yourself man? I mean, yeah, she's in a distressing situation, but no one took her story at face value? Not even you?".

Bishop sighs "I'll admit, I was feeble minded at the time. A rookie cop trying to impress the right people to jump start my career. I went against my better judgement. We had no leads and I didn't want to rock the boat. The attack looked random. But when I saw the same gash on Harvey's face, my heart sank. I knew immediately we had made a mistake. I don't care what it takes, I'm going to rectify the mistake I made in not speaking up back then. She deserves closure and so do you Jaxon. Right now, I'm working on finding a connection between Harvey and the other victim, William. I've noticed, when there's no clear reason for why something happened, there's usually secrets to uncover. You guys ask around. See if anyone knows a guy who wears a mask like that, who gashes his victims face, anything useful. I'll call you guys later with an update. I've got to get back to work".

Crowded sidewalks, concrete stoops, and glass storefront windows chock-full of advertisements line the blocks between Paisley's apartment and place of work. She nestles her coffee between her chest and forearm, juggling a half-eaten strawberry cream cheese turnover and her cell phone in one hand. The other hand tucks her earbuds into her ears and picks a playlist for her mile trek to the restaurant.

"I probably looked like a mess but I'm kind of impressed I pulled that off" she chuckles proudly to herself, placing her phone in her jacket pocket.

For today's walk, Paisley opts for a piano music

playlist to offset the chaotic scene of scurrying people and driver's hanging out of their windows shouting and shaking their impatient fists. She adores how the music can add a dramatic flair to her walks, turning insignificant happenings into mini dramas. Sometimes she even imagines a perfect life as her crime fighting, billionaire alter ego, Paisley Sinclair. Paisley Sinclair has it all together and every week, she trades the rough life of expensive champagne and caviar for kicking ass and taking names. Paisley Sinclair says what she means and means what she says. If only she were more than a figment of Paisley's imagination.

Bewitched by the music, Paisley's mind wanders "Today feels like a good day" she thinks, taking confident strides, "I think I'll stop at Joe's Pizza Shop after work. I've been craving pizza lately. Maybe I'll even surprise Londyn with her favorite Bacon Pickle Pizza. I still don't know why she likes that one, but hey, she puts up with my Mac-n-Cheese Pizza so I guess I can't complain too much".

With her workplace finally in sight, Paisley tosses the final bite of her strawberry cream cheese turnover into her mouth. She spots a trash can outside the neighboring deli and summons her alter ego as she whirls around with the intent of slamming her coffee inside. She collides with a deli customer exiting the building. Her petite frame is no match for the bear of a man. Paisley falls to the ground. Her ear buds are knocked out of her ears and the remaining contents of her coffee paints the sidewalk.

"Hey, watch it will ya!" The man grunts, wearing a frustrated glare as he walks away.

"And clumsy Paisley is back" Paisley sighs under her breath, her face crimson with embarrassment.

"Paisley, are you ok!? That man was so rude!" Macie runs over and helps Paisley to her feet.

"I'm ok, it was my fault" Paisley insists, dusting herself off.

Macie shakes her head "No, he was an asshole", she looks around Paisley, yelling at the man "Hey asshole! Watch where you're going next time! You could at least help her pick her stuff up you know!".

"Thanks Macie" Paisley's dimples accompany her smile.

The coworkers walk together.

Macie turns to Paisley "Oh, hey. I know you don't like, go out and stuff, but a few of us are going to the bar after work. You should totally come".

"Ehh, I don't know Macie" Paisley's voice apprehensive.

"Pleeeeease. Just this once and I promise I won't ask again, for like at least a month. Two months!" Macie negotiates, opening the back door to the restaurant.

"Even if I wanted to, I don't have any going out clothes" Paisley ties up her curly blonde hair.

"I've got like three dresses in my car waiting for spontaneous outings like this. We're probably the same size. I'll let you try them on after work. If they don't fit, I won't bug you about it anymore. But if they do fit, you must come out with us. Deal?" Macie grins, bouncing on her toes.

"Ok… deal" Paisley gives in, flashing a nervous smile.

A generous glass of whiskey between his palms, Jaxon sits on the kitchen counter, swinging his legs back and forth.

"Where's your head at?" Elijah asks Jaxon who's wearing a pondering stare into space.

"Have you ever known Bishop to sit back and be quiet? Not speak up when he knows something doesn't feel right?" Jaxon asks, studying an empty spot on the wall.

"I don't think so. I mean, he's always struck me as a speak-his-mind type of guy, why?" Elijah's face puzzles.

Jaxon taps his fingers on his glass of whiskey and looks at Elijah "Harvey was at the park too… when I got shot".

"Yeah" Elijah's voice waiting for Jaxon's conclusion.

Jaxon hops off the counter, continuing to piece the events together "Follow me on this. What if the hit wasn't on Miles? What if it was on Harvey? Bishop didn't do anything to warn either of us about being there. Almost like he wanted to make sure we were there when the hit took place. The girl, the only witness to her fiancé's murder, gave a distinct description of the killer's mask. Bishop did nothing with that information. Almost like he didn't want the killer to be found. He gave some sorry excuse that no one talks to the cops. People talk. Maybe not right away, but a little persistence and persuasion, someone always talks. And then, two years later, Harvey is murdered by, one can only assume, the guy with the mask. And suddenly, Bishop wants to help. Why? I know you said you reached out to him and asked, but what if he knew I was looking into Harvey's murder before you told him I was? What if he's only helping so he can keep tabs on what's known and what's not. You know, control the narrative. We're missing something, I can feel it. I don't trust him".

"Damn… That's a lot to process. I mean, in a crazy, conspiracy kind of way it sounds plausible, I guess. But Bishop? A criminal mastermind? You don't think that's a stretch?" Elijah's eyes fill with question.

"Honestly, I don't know" Jaxon's swirls his whiskey before shooting it back.

Elijah's phone rings, Bishop's smiling profile picture fills the screen. Jaxon and Elijah exchange suspicious glances.

"Hello?" Elijah answers.

## Chapter Four

*Two years ago. One month before William's murder*

DiMaggio's, a popular speakeasy style bar with live jazz music on the weekends, fills to capacity. Paisley and her friends, Londyn, Chloe, and Serenity, crowd around a sticky, dark oak table. Giddy smiles kick off their monthly girl's night outing.

"Oh my gosh, Paisley. I swear the bouncer knew your i.d. was fake!" Londyn giggles, folding her arms in front of her as she takes a seat.

"Right! I was certain he could see my heart beating out of my chest!" Paisley grabs a handful of laminated drink menus and passes them out to her friends.

"My question is, how hard did you bat your eyelashes?" Serenity teases.

"What ever do you mean?" Paisley mocks an English accent as she tilts her head towards her raised shoulder, touching it with her chin.

Serenity rolls her eyes, giving Paisley a gentle shove.

Chloe gets Londyn and Serenity's attention. She jerks her head towards a poster advertisement on the wall, and the three girls look at Paisley, waiting to see who will muster up the courage to tell her.

"What? Why are you guys looking at me like I'm a lost puppy?" Paisley laughs nervously.

Londyn reaches for Paisley's hand and holds it in hers "So, any idea why we chose to come this particular bar tonight?".

Paisley's eyes dart around the room, searching for clues "Umm... Half-priced margarita's?"

Chloe shrugs "Well... I mean, that's a plus. But not quite".

Paisley gives in, chewing at a fingernail from her

free hand "Ok, the suspense is killing me. Someone spill!".

Londyn takes in a deep breath "DiMaggio's is putting on a singing competition next weekend. We knew you would never sign yourself up. So… we signed you up. And you have until the end of the night to pick the song you want to sing".

Paisley's eyes widen, a timid look freezes her face.

Londyn continues "Before you freak out, you're an amazing singer, you know you are. Shy, bashful, but amazing. And as your best friends, it is our duty to give you the push you need to go after your dream. Don't worry, we will all be there to watch you wow everyone!"

Paisley stammers "Ok, I, umm… don't totally hate the idea. My mind is filled with so many potential"

"Songs to sing?" Serenity finishes Paisley's sentence excitedly.

"I was going to say potential ways to screw up but maybe best to think positive?" Paisley chuckles timorously "Who knew it was possible to hate you guys and love you, at the same time".

The friends laugh and order their drinks from an

approaching waiter.

Across the room, Jaxon and Bishop are seated at the bar, where their friend Caroline is bartending.

"Hey, thanks again for getting us in Caroline. You're the best bartender ever, you know that?" Jaxon leans around his menu flashing a sly grin.

"Always the charmer aren't you Jax? That grin isn't getting you guys free drinks though" Caroline smirks as she garnishes a finished cocktail.

"Come on, just one!?" He hollers, watching Caroline walk the drink over to a thirsty customer.

Jaxon turns his attention to Bishop "You know what I just realized?".

"You like Caroline?" Bishop's tone playfully bantering.

Jaxon twists in his chair, throwing a joking side-eye at Bishop "No bro. Well, yeah, I like her. But that's not what I was about to say".

"Just ask her out already man" Bishop interrupts, crunching on a bar nut.

"Dude, tonight is about you, not me. Now stay on topic here" Jaxon snickers softly "this time next week, you'll be out patrolling the streets of New York".

"Yeah, but with a veteran who probably won't even let me think about driving" Bishop complains, resting his arm atop the bar.

"You never know, some people hate driving. Harvey for example. He's the older brother, yet every time we go somewhere, I gotta drive" Jaxon rolls his eyes.

The two friends order beers, celebratory double bourbon shots, and continue talking.

Minutes turn into hours, full glasses of alcohol continually replace empty ones, and conversations climb a few drunk decibels higher than before.

"Where did our waiter go?... You know what, I'm just going to go order our shots from the bart instead" Paisley shoots up, stumbling drunkenly over her own foot.

"I'm ok" she stammers, raising her hands for balance.

Londyn leans her back against the chair and grabs hold of Paisley's passing arm "Wait up, one of us should go with you".

"No, I need you girls to keep looking at songs. You have to help me figure out the perfect song for next week" Paisley pleads, pouting her merlot colored lips.

"Ok, ok. We got you covered" Serenity assures, a corner of her mouth quirks up.

On an alcohol fueled mission, Paisley stumbles through the crowd. A couple, dressed to the nines, gives Paisley a dirty look as she leans her palm on their wobbly table trying to collect herself. She moves her curly hair away from her face and takes a deep breath as the fruity cocktails and multiple vodka shots are taking over her system. Paisley focuses her glossy eyes on a group of guys antagonizing a pale, dark-haired gentleman near the corner bathrooms.

"Just ignore them" She tells herself.

The timid man is pushed to the alcohol puddled floor and Paisley's bleeding-heart compels her.

She pushes through the crowd and before she knows it, she's standing right behind the rowdy group.

"Hey! What's your problem? Leave him alone!" Her voice battles the loud jazz music.

The trembling man looks on as the towering men turn their scruffy faces towards Paisley.

"Such bravery, such... beauty" he admires under his breath.

"Ok, probably not the brightest idea Paisley" she thinks, nervously standing her ground.

Although her heart races her breathes on the inside, her intent stare on the outside is enough to convince the group to move on.

"Oh, thank goodness" she closes her eyes with a sigh of relief.

Paisley extends a hand to help the clean-shaven man off the floor.

"Thanks for doing that. I don't know how you found the courage to stand up to such animals, but I'm glad you did. My name is Willard. And you are?" Willard smooths down his jacket.

"Paisley. You're welcome Willard. Yeah, my

friends tell me my tenderhearted nature will get me in trouble someday. Maybe they're right, but I just don't have it in me to sit and do nothing when bad things happen" Paisley smiles humbly.

Willard reciprocates a smile.

"Be safe out there Willard" Paisley raises a hand in farewell and begins to walk away.

"I won't forget you or your kindness Paisley" Willard's quiet voice barely reaches Paisley's eardrums.

Paisley stops half a second, taken aback by the ominous feeling that swept over her as he muttered those words. She looks back over her shoulder. Willard leans against the wall, gazing at her.

She quickly turns back around, bumping drunkenly into a decorative plant.

"Something about his face or the look in his eyes or… I don't really know what it is, but something doesn't feel right. I don't know, maybe it's the alcohol" She dismisses the eerie feeling as she returns to her original mission of ordering shots.

Jaxon's night comes to an end as he and Bishop stumble outside and say their farewells.

Jaxon nears an abandoned building a block from the bar, where he hears laughing and jesting.

"Sounds like someone's about to get their ass kicked" Jaxon scoffs, glancing down the littered alley as a man is thrown against a locked back door.

The man falls to the ground, knocking a wooden crate full of glass bottles over.

The man scrambles to grab a broken bottle to use as a weapon.

"Your little girlfriend isn't here to save you this time" a burly man sneers, kicking the bottle towards the grounded man.

Glass shatters against the brick building, sending shards violently into the grounded man's face. He winces as blood begins to drip rapidly.

The other two men mock the victim's pain.

"Damn it" Jaxon sighs under his breath, knowing he's about to get involved.

He grabs a two by four from a nearby dumpster.

"One good hit and big bear is down for the

count" he thinks.

Jaxon creeps up quietly, dodging muddy puddles on the ground. Close enough now, he swings the board with all his might, knocking the rugged man from standing to lying in a pile of garbage bags. The other two men turn around and square up. Jaxon can see their wheels turning, debating what their plan of attack should be.

"I wouldn't" Jaxon's baseball stance hints his first swing wasn't just a lucky shot.

In sync, both men rush Jaxon. He swings again, breaking the board over the second man's head. The third strikes Jaxon and both men come to a standoff.

Jaxon spits a mouthful of blood "Come on gym muscles, that all you got?"

Before the man can respond Jaxon's adrenaline drive's him forward. His squared shoulders lay into the man's chest sending both against the wall. The man's head bounces off the brick, tossing him into a daze. Jaxon's fists rain into his face, knocking him to the cracked pavement.

With each man no longer a threat, Jaxon helps the bloodied man off the ground "Hey man, I'm Jaxon. You alright?".

"I will be, I'm Willard" Willard coughs, grabbing his rib area, "Wow, you just took out three men. You've got a knack for fighting, haven't you?".

Drunk, eyes half open, Jaxon grins "Where I'm from, you either learn to defend yourself or you may as well paint a target on your back".

Willard rubs his clean-shaven chin "Quite the philosophy. Anyways, so these men… what do you say we make them disappear, huh?".

Jaxon wears a puzzled expression "Wait, what do you mean disappear? Like murder?"

Willard shrugs, a cold look in his eyes and a hollowness in his voice "They would've murdered me had you not stepped in. You know, you're the second person to help me tonight. Although you look more the part of a fighter, I was shown that courage can come in small packages too. I am that small package right now".

Jaxon pats Willard's shoulder "Murder isn't courage Willard. Don't let TV fool you, murder is more permanent than you may think it is".

Expressionless, Willard stares at the men, imagining how their deaths would play out.

Sensing an eerie disappointment on the part of

Willard, Jaxon decides it is time to bid him goodbye "Look, just be careful alright, there's a lot of bad people out there".

"I won't soon forget you Jaxon" a slightly perturbed Willard hollers out at Jaxon walking away.

His back towards Willard, Jaxon puts his hand up in farewell "Alright man" he thinks.

## *Present Day*

Elijah takes a seat on the worn wooden park bench "Any idea why Bishop wants to meet? He was pretty vague on the phone call".

Jaxon leans on the park bench and mocks Bishop's voice "Meet me at the park in half an hour", Jaxon scoffs "Why? So, you know where to send your hitman? I don't know, we just met with him this morning, there's no way he caught a break in the case already. Unless he's in on it".

"In on what?" Bishop approaches from behind, a bag of bagels in one hand, a manila envelope in the other.

Jaxon and Elijah look at each other and then back at Bishop.

"In on what?" Bishop pushes curiously, "wait before you answer that, I brought two peace offerings. Cinnamon bagels from Lou's Bakery and proof my rookie ass was in over my head the night you got shot. I knew if I told you that on the phone, you probably would have told me to screw myself... so, here we are".

"Jaxon thinks you're a criminal mastermind" Elijah blurts out, growing tired of the tension between the two former friends.

Jaxon shoots a mystified look at Elijah "Wow, bro. Just throw all our cards down on the table why don't ya".

"What? He brought cinnamon bagels from Lou's, Jax. Cinnamon bagels from Lou's are the Brooklyn version of humble pie. Plus, you said it yourself, it's out of character for Bishop to sit back when something bad is happening" Elijah contends, shrugging and grabbing a bagel from Bishop.

Bishop laughs uncontrollably "Criminal mastermind? And what, do I have a secret lair filled with all of my failed plans for taking over the world too? I mean, I'm flattered Jaxon, but you must realize how ridiculous that sounds, right?".

Jaxon looks Bishop in the eyes. He knew Bishop better than anyone, at least he used to. Right now, Jaxon sees a familiar glimmer of hope on Bishop's face. He's had his guard up for two years though. It's not going to be so easily torn down, but Jaxon is assured enough to at least hear Bishop's proof of his saving grace.

Jaxon scoffs lightly, playing off his suspicion and grabbing a bagel from the bag "I wasn't a hundred percent serious about the accusation".

Bishop jokingly shakes his head, composing his chuckles "alright, so I've got a recording I want you to listen to. It's from that night, in my squad car. I was wearing a wire. They called it… an audition to keep my job. You remember how I was so worried about getting stuck with a partner who wouldn't let me drive?".

Jaxon nods, crumbs falling to the ground as he takes a bite of sweet cinnamon deliciousness.

Bishop continues "Well, I would have rather got stuck with a partner like that than the one I got. I was a rookie cop riding around with a dirty one. Not for long though. Before they placed me with him, there were suspicions he was working the blocks, getting a piece of the profits from drug deals. Long as dealers gave him a share, they were free to do business on his watch. He had been riding solo for a long time, that's how he was able to get away with it. So, obviously he didn't take it too well when he got stuck with a partner. Now, Miles, well you guys knew Miles, so I don't have to tell you that he was a dealer. But what you probably didn't know, was his desire to get out of the drug game. He wanted to get clean. My partner, paranoid asshole that he was, figured Miles would snitch on him for being dirty cop. So, he put a hit on him disguised as a drug deal gone bad. But of course, he couldn't tell his new partner that. He probably figured I'd turn him in too, and he would've been right. Little did he know; he was already being investigated. The day of the shooting, I was advised nothing can be out of the ordinary or my partner will get suspicious. And he would have. I swear if the birds didn't sing the right way, that dude was on high alert. While they set me up with the wire, they told me about the hit on Miles, but it was hear say. They needed concrete proof. My job was to get my partner talking about it somehow and then they'd swoop in and arrest him before the hit even took place. All the puzzle pieces would fall in line. It was risky, yeah, but to get a dirty cop off the streets, I guess they thought it was worth it. Well, my dialogue wasn't convincing enough and the information we were fed wasn't accurate either. The hit was an hour earlier than expected. As soon as the hitman pulled up to take out Miles, everything hit the fan. My partner cuffs my hand to the steering wheel, shots ring out, sirens wail, and tires screech. I look over and see you falling to the ground, clutching your stomach. The look in your eyes when you saw me just sitting there helpless to help you. I'll never forget that. All I could think about was how I let you die. It was the worst night of my life".

Elijah wipes the side of his crumb crusted mouth "Wow, talk about a rough start".

Bishop opens the envelope "Tell me about it. Anyways, I didn't come here to give you my sob story. I made you a copy of the wiretap, Jaxon. Just listen to it when you get the chance. Maybe it'll give you the confidence in me you used to have".

Jaxon accepts the flash drive from Bishop "Alright, I'll listen to it. That's a shady deal they gave you. Sucks you had to go through that. I do have one question though. Why reach out and help now?".

"When I saw Harvey was murdered by the same

guy from two years ago, it reminded me that twice I went against my better judgement. Once by not taking that girl's story seriously and twice by not warning you and Harvey about the danger you were in. I figured I'd better start listening to my conscience again. Squash the beef with you and catch this killer once and for all" Bishop answers.

Jaxon and Bishop share a handshake and a look of copacetic understanding.

Paisley washes up, waiting on Macie to return with the dresses she hopes won't fit her.

"Yeah right, you're not that lucky" she thinks, gazing musingly at herself through the water spotted bathroom mirror.

Macie bursts through the door, sending it against the tiled wall.

"Oh my gosh! You about gave me a heart attack" Paisley gasps.

Macie laughs giddily "Sorry, I'm just excited. That or my second energy drink just kicked in. Either way, here. Try these on".

Paisley's eyes widen, a flush creeps up her face "Macie, these are too sexy! Do you not have anything less… revealing?".

"Is that a trick question?" Macie smirks mischievously, "Just try them on. You promised, Paisley".

"Ok, ok, you're right" Paisley drapes the dresses around her arm and enters the bathroom stall riddled with marker written messages and etched doodles.

After giving each dress the college try, she settles on a laced, open back bodycon dress.

Paisley gives the dress and her hair one last adjustment before she pushes the wedged stall door open and steps out "so… how do I look?"

Macie's voice jumps an excited octave "Girl! You look great! You totally rock my dress better than I do! Kinda jealous actually".

A humble smile crosses Paisley's face.

"Are you sure you don't want me to just pick up some extra shifts for you guys or something?" Paisley tries her luck at weaseling out of going.

"Paisley, if you take anymore shifts, they're going to start charging you rent" Macie teases.

Paisley giggles softly, accompanied by a half-smile.

Macie wraps her arm around Paisley's shoulder "Come on, it'll be fun"

"Ugh, it's only been one hour? Really? Why does time only fly when you're having fun?" Paisley thinks, sipping the rest of her watered-down Old Fashioned.

She spaces out, watching her coworkers' genuine smiles and joyful conversations. Paisley runs her finger around the rim of her empty glass, her chin resting in her palm.

"I think I need a stronger drink" she thinks, scooting her chair out and standing up.

"Hey, do you guys need anything? I'm going to order from the bar this time" Paisley pushes her chair back in.

"Shots? Can we please do vodka this time guys?" Macie pleads, pouting her lips.

The group agree on vodka shots.

Paisley navigates the empty tables and small

crowds of people on the way to the bar.

Her heart flutters as she notices a familiar face sitting at the bar; Jaxon.

He sits observing a flash drive, a blank look on his face.

"Hey stranger. I owe you a drink for saving me the other night" Paisley wears the first smile of the night she didn't have to force.

Jaxon turns, the smell of perfume singing a sexy song to his nose.

He tucks the flash drive away, smiling back "Oh hey! I'm just glad it worked. It would have been pretty deflating had it not" he laughs.

Paisley tucks a curl behind her ear, her beautiful doe-eyes find comfort in his alluring gaze.

She extends her hand "I'm Paisley by the way. I realized we never exchanged names the other night".

Jaxon embraces Paisley's hand in his, her fingertips gentle like the petals of roses "I'm Jaxon. It's nice to officially meet you Paisley. So, uh, what brings you out tonight?".

Paisley twists and points towards her coworkers,

playfully bantering at their corner table "I got dragged out by well-meaning coworkers, how about you?".

Jaxon sets his beer down on a coaster "I just came to clear my mind after meeting with a former best friend".

Paisley takes an empty seat next to Jaxon "Sounds like neither of us are truly here on our own accord".

"Cheers to that" Jaxon scoffs gently, "so, you said they had to drag you out? Why'd they have to drag you?".

Paisley orders another Old Fashioned and a beer for Jaxon from the bartender "I don't really like being out and about anymore. Crowds, groups of people, they make me nervous. Sometimes my anxiety just completely takes over. I feel my lungs forgetting how to breath, the walls close in on me, and fainting feels like the only way out".

Jaxon takes a sip of beer "Damn, if I felt like that, I don't know if I would want to be out either. There a story behind that? If you don't mind me asking of course".

Paisley gives a dismissive wave, her sweet, husky voice draws Jaxon in "You're ok, my best friend says I should talk about it with someone instead of bottling it up. I've tried, but I guess bottling is easier… Anyways, umm, two years ago, I saw my fiancé get murdered. He was stabbed to death right in front of me. I stood there, frozen with fear and sure the killer was coming for me next. But instead, he just looked at me for a minute and took off. They never did catch the guy. The police swore it was random. Regardless, I was never given the chance to know why it happened. Now it's like… when I see people, when they look at me, when they talk to me, I feel like their intentions are bad. I battle these thoughts in my head that I'm going to be murdered or kidnapped or something. On top of that, lately, I've been getting this strange feeling I'm being watched. Everyone says it's just in my head, but I don't know. Maybe it is, maybe I'm going crazy?" Paisley scoffs gently, "I feel like these past two years, my life is this perfect storm of misery and things going wrong, mixed with waves of happiness here and there".

A corner of Jaxon's mouth lifts, he rubs his chiseled jaw "Well, you don't strike me as crazy. That's a traumatic experience to go through. I mean, it's tough when you lose someone that way. I'm sorry to hear about your fiancé. My brother was murdered as well, a couple weeks ago. And ever since then, I guess I've been in denial because this is the first time I'm going to admit this, but I've began to spiral downward into this pit of anger and alcohol. I blame myself for what happened. Him and I got into an argument after I caused a scene at the club the night he was murdered. He left, I stayed. Next thing I know, he's gone. If I would have been there walking home with him, I'm certain he wouldn't have been a victim".

Paisley swirls her ice with her straw "I'm sorry to hear about your brother. Unfortunately, I know how hard that must be. You mentioned you met with a former best friend. Why former?".

Jaxon grabs his beer and takes another swig "Two years ago, I was playing basketball at the park when a hit on a drug dealer we were playing with took place. I got caught in the crossfire. Took three shots and almost died right there in the middle of the court. My best friend had just become a cop not long before that. While I was falling to the ground, I saw him just sitting in his squad car. Cops were all over the place, but he just sat there, eyes wide like he'd never seen a shooting before. What's more is, I found out he knew about the hit. He knew the danger I was in by being there. He never warned me, and he didn't get out to help. Because of that, a part of me felt betrayed. But, today was the first time in two years I second guessed my decision. I guess it should feel good, right? But I cut my best friend out of my life for two years and I'm realizing it may have been the wrong thing to do. What kind of friend am I if I find out he couldn't have done a thing?".

"For what it's worth, you seem like a pretty good guy Jaxon. We're all human, we make mistakes. You helped me the other night. I was a complete stranger. You didn't have to go out of your way for me, but you did. It was sweet. You even gave me a compliment that night and although I could tell you felt like it was an awkward compliment, it wasn't. It was something I needed to hear" Paisley places her hand on the back of Jaxon's hand.

Jaxon's heart warms, he smiles at Paisley "Thank you. You know, if you ever need some company, you're always welcome in 6F".

Paisley draws the corner of her bottom lip between her teeth and returns a gentle smile "I'll probably take you up on that. You're always welcome in 4A".

Paisley's text alert dings "Sorry, my friends are probably wondering where their shots are.

Her heart skips a beat as she stares at a picture of her and Jaxon talking, and an unopened audio message delivered by a blocked number.

Another text comes in from the blocked number "listen with Jaxon".

Paisley breathes shakily as she shows Jaxon and they prepare to open the audio message together. They take deep breaths and press play.

Willard let's out an admiring sigh "how sweet it is to see my two favorite people getting to know one another". Jaxon and Paisley wear puzzled expressions as they glance around the room, trying to figure out who sent the message. Willard's hollow voice continues, "I know, I know, you're probably thinking "who is this?". Well… you see guys, herein lies the problem. Two years of supermarket conversations, passing hello's in the park, clanking beers together in the bar, polite smiles as we moved passed one another on a busy subway. Paisley you've waited on me at the restaurant. Jaxon you've spotted me in the gym. Yet, I am fully convinced neither of you have a lick of remembrance of me or the night we met. Were you really that drunk? Maybe it's me. I'm used to blending in and going unnoticed. But that night, something happened that had never happened before. Someone noticed me, two someone's. Your precious hearts stepped in and saved me. But how quickly you both forgot me. I see it in your eyes every time you look at me. I didn't forget you though. I even returned the favor. Paisley, I'm sorry I had to kill William, but he wasn't who you thought he was. He couldn't give you the happy life a tender heart like yours deserves. Jaxon, I'm sorry I had to kill Harvey. He was bringing you down again. I couldn't sit back and do nothing this time. Don't you see? I saved you guys. But I don't see gratefulness on your faces. Just sorrow and unhappiness. It pains me that the two people who made me feel important two years ago, have made me feel insignificant and, again invisible ever since. There is an upside, well for me anyways. You want to know the best thing about going through life unnoticed?... You, the police, no one will suspect me. So, when I keep killing to see how much death your bleeding hearts can handle, you'll all be none the wiser. Insert maniacal laugh here for dramatic effect. Wait, I wasn't supposed to read that, I was supposed to laugh maniacally. Oh well, that's ruined. Anyways, I'll watch you later guys. Keep your friends and family close.".

## Chapter Five

Falling asleep was starting to seem like an impossible task. Paisley tosses and turns, covering up and cuddling her blanket one minute, sprawling out and tossing it off the next. She watches the mesmerizing rotation of particleboard blades, spacing out to the familiar hum of her ceiling fan. The thoughts in her head run into each other as the reality of her situation begins to close in.

"Who was that guy? Was he really William's killer? What did he mean when he said I saved him? If what he said had any truth to it, that means… I've been face to face with a cold-blooded murderer" her pupils dilate, her heartbeat quickens as her throat dries "That is a frightening thought. I've talked with, smiled at, even waited on a murderer".

Thirty stunned seconds go by before she gives in, throwing her warm blanket off once more "Welp, so much for sleeping".

Paisley grabs her plush, Carolina blue robe from her vanity chair and slips into it, hugging herself for added warmth. The cold floor creaks beneath her feet as she makes her way to the kitchen cupboard, reaching for a porcelain bowl.

"Frosted Loops or Cookie Crunch?" She ponders, rubbing her tired eyes.

She chooses the familiar comfort of Cookie Crunch. While most people reach for ice cream, Cookie Crunch was Paisley's go to. She smiles softly as she imagines Londyn teasing her for choosing cereal over ice cream. No matter how hard Londyn tried to change her mind, Paisley always found that crunching on little chocolaty cookies was the more heartening choice.

She tips the box of cereal. A rush of barley corn grains slides quickly into her bowl, several rogue pieces opting for the kitchen counter.

"Keep your friends and family close" Willard's hollow warning echoes in her head as she goes to grab milk from the refrigerator.

Paisley takes in a sharp breath when a fleeting flashback of him staring at her through his mask replays in her head. She glances over her shoulder at her dark, empty apartment. Without warning, the sound of silence gives her the shivers. Paisley turns back around, her eyes focus on a bottle of red wine. She wrestles with the idea of taking Jaxon up on his offer of company. In just the little amount of time she'd spent in his presence, she felt a sense of security that had never graced her before.

"It's the middle of the night Paisley" she thinks, softly biting her fingernail "But maybe he can't sleep either? The guy on the phone did target him too… But IT'S THE MIDDLE OF THE NIGHT" she stresses the detail again to herself.

Paisley shakes her head, ignoring the idea. There is no way she's going over there at a time like this. Instead, she fills her spoon with milk and mini cookies. A vibrating weather alert on her phone breaks the eerie silence, causing her to jump. The motion transfers the milk and cereal from her spoon to the kitchen counter.

Paisley can't help but slap her palm to her forehead and giggle.

She sighs, rolling her eyes light heartedly "Ok... sorry Cookie Crunch. Wine and a chance it is".

She throws her long, curly hair into a high ponytail, slides her feet into cozy slippers, and grabs the wine and two wide-bottomed glasses.

As she closes her front door, Paisley leans her back against it and takes a deep, thinking breath "worst case scenario, he thinks you're crazy, never wants to see you again, and you're alone like you already are... Ok, nice pep talk... You've really got to work at this whole, positivity thing".


Lounging on his microfiber couch, Jaxon's TV watches him as he's lost in thought "Damn, why don't I remember this dude? Nothing about his voice or his story sounds even remotely familiar. And".

A knock at the door interrupts his thoughts. Jaxon's eyebrows draw together as he wonders if the guy on the phone would try such a brazen attack.

Jaxon creeps quietly towards his door, stepping around a pile of laundry and the empty pizza box he's been ignoring.

He places his eye against the peephole "Shit!" he thinks as he sees Paisley standing patiently behind the door.

Jaxon frantically tries to make his apartment look more presentable, kicking the pizza box under the couch and tossing the pile of laundry inside his coat closet. In his mind, he can see Morgan giving him an I-told-you-so look. Her frequent instruction of keeping his apartment guest ready is looking like million-dollar advice right about now. He throws empty beer bottles from his cluttered kitchen counter to the trash can and pulls on a white t-shirt, careful not to mess up his hair.

He opens the door, a welcoming smile on his face "Hey Paisley".

"Hey, umm… so, I was wondering if your offer still stands? Even though it's the middle of the night" A corner of Paisley's mouth lifts as she nervously presents a bottle of wine and two glasses with a half shrug.

"Yeah of course, come on in" Jaxon moves aside and closes the door behind Paisley.

"I'm sorry it's so late, I hope I'm not intruding"

Paisley wears an apologetic expression as the two crowd the kitchen counter.

"Nah, you're good. I'm usually up late these days. Everything ok? Besides the obvious of course" Jaxon pulls out a wine opener and begins opening the bottle.

"Yeah, no I'm fine, I just couldn't sleep. I keep replaying that spine-chilling message in my head. The more I tried to keep my mind from wandering to over-the-top ways I could be murdered, the more ominous my apartment got" Paisley crosses her arms over her chest and sighs.

Jaxon pulls the cork out and pours Paisley a glass of Pinot Noir and then one for himself "Would you like to talk about it? Or do you prefer blissful ignorance tonight?".

Paisley accepts the glass from Jaxon as the two make their way to his couch "Blissful ignorance with a side of my life is normal?" She giggles softly.

Jaxon chuckles "I'll have the same. So, what's your story? How'd you end up here at Kent Gardens?".

Paisley takes a sip of her crushed grapes and crosses her legs "Well, if you can believe it, I'm not originally from New York. My elementary years, I was a small-town girl from Georgia with a cherry popsicle stained grin and not a care in the world. I was an only child, but I liked that. We were happy, always smiling. Family dinners around the table every night, playing on the swing set while the enticing smell of homemade apple pie lingered from an open kitchen window. Tucked in with bedtime stories and kisses goodnight. I felt like… my life was perfect. But… I guess my parents didn't think so. Right before my first year of middle school started, they seized an opportunity and we picked up and moved to New York".

"Damn, I can imagine that was quite a culture shock" Jaxon raises his brows as he rests his arm atop the armrest.

Paisley nods and continues "Oh my gosh, it was! I had a hard time adjusting. Not to mention, we were just in time for me to start a week late. I was that shy, quiet new girl who didn't quite fit in with any specific crowd. So, I just wrapped my sixth-grade hands around my backpack straps and huddled through the halls every day, eyes fixed on the floor. Fast forward to high school and all that changed. I took up singing and I could have never imagined how that decision would change my life. It was just a hobby; I wasn't supposed to be good at it. Singing just… I guess it just let me escape the world. I could shut everything and everyone out and just be that little girl running around the meadow, picking flowers again" Paisley smiles gently as she reminisces, "The first few years of high school, I was suddenly popular. Not in a queen of the school kind of way, but people actually wanted to be my friend. My confidence was high, I was entering and winning singing competitions, it was nice".

Paisley hesitates, staring at her lipstick stained wine glass as she presses a finger against her bottom lip "And then… again, life changed. The summer before my senior year, I took a trip back to my hometown to visit old friends and walk down memory lane. Two weeks later, when I came back home to New York, my life was gone. A fire took everything away. My house, my parents" Paisley stops and takes a deep breath, tears glistening in her eyes as Jaxon comfortingly rubs her back, "I went to live with my best friend Londyn, and by the time senior year started, I was back to middle school me. I shut people away. I quit singing. If it hadn't been for Londyn, I don't know how or if I would have been able to pull myself together. A few weeks before William was taken from me, I entered and won my first singing competition since the fire. Then, when I lost him soon after that, I started to lose myself again. This time I vowed I wouldn't stop singing. So, I moved to Kent Gardens since it was a few blocks from the art district where I practiced. And over the last two years I've been singing random gigs all over town. Speaking of random gigs, I have one tomorrow night at Mo's. If you're not doing anything, I hear they have the best steak in Brooklyn?".

Jaxon's mouth curves into a smile, a look of beaming admiration in his eyes "Looks like I'll be checking out the steak at Mo's tomorrow. You know… You're an impressive girl Paisley. I imagine your parents would be proud of you and what you've accomplished".

"Thank you, Jaxon" Paisley's heart flutters, her cheeks turning pink as she grins, turns her face away, and tucks a loose curl behind her ear.

Her emerald eyes take up residence in his "What about you, what's your story?".

Jaxon rubs his shoulder "Umm, I'm a Brooklyn native. My brother, sister, and I had an adventurous childhood to say the least. Jumping in the water plug, playing stickball until the streetlights lit up, block parties, and running around with the neighborhood hard-knocks. My parents worked hard to keep us out of the streets and out of trouble", Jaxon chuckles softly "I don't know who was more intimidating, my mom or my dad. He was an associate to a foot soldier in the mob. He didn't think we knew, but he was the muscle, not the brains. My mom, she was from Jersey and when she got going, that Jersey accent was coming at you quick. We could always tell how much trouble we were in by how strong her accent was".

Paisley crinkles her nose, giggling as Jaxon continues "I was the sporty sibling. I had this dream I'd be a star baseball player, and through elementary school, I was. At ten years old, my father's mafia connections landed him in jail for twenty years. I remember before they took him away, he looked me in the eyes and said "Jackie, be better than me". It hit me the hardest when he was gone but it was tough for all of us. My mom worked two jobs to keep the lights on and food on the table. Christmases and birthdays missed us more often than not. She never would have told us, but I knew she was struggling. The hours she worked started getting longer and longer. So, I started hustling. I made these little sculptures out of rocks and melted crayons. The kids at school loved them, so I started selling them. My mom never would've taken money from her children. She was too proud. So, every Friday night I'd gather all the money I'd made, sneak into her room, and hide the money in her purse. It wasn't much, but it felt good to help out".

"That is so sweet and creative. How awesome that you were able to find a way to help out at such a young age" Paisley's eyes light up with astonishment.

Jaxon flashes a humble smile "Thank you. I remember I came home from school one day and my mom about beat my ass. I don't know how she found out, but she'd heard I was selling rocks at school. She thought I was selling drugs" Jaxon cracks up laughing, "When I told her I was creating these little rock sculptures and selling them, she didn't believe me. So, I got my materials out, sat on the floor, and showed her. When she saw the care and the work I put into each one, she got down on her knees, hugged me, and cried. She was so proud. From then on, she told me to save what I made until I got to high school, that way I could afford to play baseball again. So, I did, and I was a baseball star all through high school. With every win, came a party. And with parties, came heavy drinking and fighting. Other kids, they could drink on the weekend and be good until the next. But me, I guess I developed my dad's taste for alcohol. It got to the point where I was drunk ninety percent of the time. I hit a turning point after I nearly beat a guy to death in a blacked-out rage. I was at a house party and this guy was wasted. He had been hitting on a friend of mine, Brighton. She wasn't interested and he didn't handle rejection well. She and I were standing with our circle of friends and the guy purposely bumps into her and calls her a whore. I saw red and went off. I know if I hadn't been drunk, I wouldn't have beat him to the point I did. I was lucky he didn't press charges or even worse, die. My sister, Morgan, was pissed when she heard about it. She was pregnant with my niece at the time. She told me she would kill me if I wasn't around to watch my niece grow up. I guess from then on, I didn't feel the need for the mask of alcohol. I didn't completely give it up, but I minimized my drinking quite a bit. A year after I graduated high school, I moved here to Kent Gardens. The plan; I'd attend the art school that is… Actually, it's right across the street from where you practice".

"Oh yeah, that building is beautiful!" Paisley moves to a side saddle position.

"Yeah it is!… I never did get around to applying though. Soon after I moved here and got all settled in, Harvey lost his job. I had him move in with me and… I don't know, I guess time just kinda flew by. I watched Bishop achieve his dream of becoming a cop, I got shot and almost died, I lost my ambition for creativity, Harvey was murdered, and now I've been leaning on that familiar crutch of alcohol and fighting. I suppose I'll get to applying someday" Jaxon plaster's a contempt expression on his face.

"Just remember, there are seven days in the week. Someday isn't one of them" Paisley encourages.

Jaxon chuckles softly, rubbing the side of his neck "You're right, you're right".

Paisley nibbles on her bottom lip "It was advice my parents gave me before I took singing seriously. I was a major procrastinator. That or I was just anxious to take the next step. I talked about singing for crowds and maybe recording my own album someday. It helped me take the steps I needed… maybe it'll help you too".

Jaxon smiles, a beam in his eyes "Hey, I've got an idea. So, you mentioned homemade apple pie earlier. Have you ever had homemade cinnamon apple chips?".

Paisley finishes her glass of wine, an intrigued look in her eyes "I have not, but they sound delicious. Apple anything takes me right back to my Georgia farmhouse".

"Perfect! I've got a recipe I've been waiting to try. It takes about an hour. I would be happy to make some, if you're not in a hurry" Jaxon rises from his seated position.

"I would love that. I'm not in a hurry at all" Paisley cozies on the couch, pulling the sleeves of her robe over her hands and wrapping her arms around herself.

Jaxon hands her the remote "Alright, cinnamon apple chips coming right up. You can turn the channel to anything you want by the way. I've just got it on baseball reruns".

Jaxon gathers his ingredients and materials, thinking to himself as he gets started "What a beautiful way to end the night. She has a soothing presence. I don't know that someone like me deserves someone like her, but…".

His thoughts are interrupted as Paisley hollers gently from the couch "Hey Jaxon?".

Jaxon looks up from slicing apples "What's up?".

She hesitates "Have you ever been stabbed?".

Jaxon looks down at his kitchen knife grasped in his hand "Yes I have".

"What does it feel like?" Paisley's nervously curious mind wanders, not sure if she really wants to know.

Jaxon looks over at Paisley, her chin resting in her palm, a glossy look in her eyes. He sees the worry on her face.

"It's not as scary as you think. But you're not ever going to find out so, you'll just have to take my word for it" Jaxon reassures, a corner of his mouth quirks up.

Paisley yawns, her voice softening "I hope not… I'm not ready to die".

Jaxon puts the final touches on the apples before placing them in the oven. A comforting cinnamon apple scent fills his apartment.

He moves from around the counter "How would you feel about…", he stops short of finishing his sentence.

Jaxon smiles sweetly as he notices Paisley has fallen asleep. Her head nestled against the cushioned armrest, she looked peacefully angelic. Jaxon retrieves an extra blanket from his linen closet.

He covers her with the blanket and as she snuggles it up to her neck, he whispers "I won't let you die Paisley"

Bishop studies the missing person's photo again, popping the rest of his chocolate muffin into his mouth. A freckle-faced twenty-one-year-old brunette with a Cheshire Cat grin plastered on her face.

"Where are you?" Bishop thinks.

He pulls out his buzzing cell phone, tapping the green answer button "What's up Captain?... Yeah, I've been out since six o'clock this morning... Ok, let me finish up with this last house and I'll be right there".

Bishop hangs up the phone as he enters the small, unlocked, white picket fenced area to a rundown home. The screen door on its' hinges, cracked windows, weeds overrunning the flower beds. Compared to the other homes in the area, this home looked out of place.

"No officer, I haven't seen anything" he mocks the answer he's been receiving all morning as he approaches the front door, knocking a nice loud detective knock.

A minute goes by. A peculiar gentleman pulls back his curtains, a blank look on his face as he gives Bishop a once over.

The gentleman slowly creaks the door open "Can I help you officer?".

Bishop pulls out the missing person's photo and flashes his badge "Yes you can. My name is Detective Kent. This girl went missing from her home around the corner two days ago. Have you seen her or anything suspicious in the area the past couple of days? Anyone or anything that doesn't belong here".

The man takes hold of the picture, studying it closely "Nope, just you officer".

Bishop's brows draw together as the man's response and cold tone stirs in his stomach "It's detective".

"Well, I'm sorry I couldn't be of more assistance officer. I mean, detective. I do hope you find the girl before something awful happens" the man begins to shut the door.

Bishop scratches his chin, trying to think of a clever scheme "You know uh… what's your name sir?".

"Willard" Willard stops short of getting the door fully shut.

Bishop tries looking inside Willard's home.

"You know Willard, it's standard procedure to search some residences, just to be sure she's not, you know, hiding out or something. You look like a fellow who values your safety. I wonder if you'd allow me to come in and check the place out, make sure you're not being held against your will or something. You know, just in case she's on the run and not just missing" Bishop internally rolls his eyes as his improv reasoning sounds ridiculous, but it's seven o'clock in the morning, his creative mind has only just woken up.

Willard cracks a suspicious smirk; a slight arrogance enters his voice "Standard procedure hmm?... Oh, I should think not detective. Have I said something to warrant suspicion? I do apologize if I have, I certainly would not have meant to".

Bishop takes a second before giving up his failing charade "You know what Willard. You have a nice day. If you see anything suspicious in the area, you give me a call alright?" Bishop hands Willard his card.

As Bishop walks away, Willard tucks the

business card in his pocket and returns inside "Now, where were we" he mumbles to himself, making his way to a padlocked door.

Willard takes out a small key, unlocks the dirty padlock, and follows his worn wooden steps to a poorly lit basement. He steps around a cardboard box and grabs a plastic chair, propping it in front of a sturdy, makeshift jail cell.

Willard grabs a bottle of water from a ripped open case on the floor and rapidly shakes a dinner bell "Wakey, wakey!".

Behind the bars, the missing brunette wakes from an uncomfortable slumber.

"Well Serenity, your disappearance, while not record breaking quick, was nonetheless noticed quickly. We just had an unexpected visitor wanting to know all about you and your whereabouts" Willard gleams with excitement, "admittedly a little too close for comfort but my adrenaline is off the charts and boy is it a thrill!".

Serenity moves to a seated position on the cot, her voice confused, tired, and annoyed "Why are you doing this? Why can't you just let me go? I haven't done anything to you. I don't even know you".

Willard's pale face goes expressionless "Oh dear Serenity, you're right. You've done nothing. But long ago, there was something you should've done. Or rather, shouldn't have done. I must say though, your lack of fear in this situation is rather... buzz killing".

Serenity shrugs.

Willard throws his hands in the air "In any case, we've got business to attend to. That's a beautiful name by the way. Serenity" Willard says her name again, this time with an elegant flair "Is that what William found in you? Peace, calm... tranquility? I mean, Paisley could have provided that, could she not? What was it in you, that made William stray?".

Serenity looks on dumbfounded thoughts clouding her mind "Who is this guy? How did he know Paisley? She couldn't have known about William's infidelity; she was too naïve back then. Even if she had, she wouldn't seek revenge".

Willard let's out a disappointed sigh "And where is Chloe these days? Oh, don't worry your pretty face with that, I've got a knack for finding people. She's just as wrong as you are Serenity. She should be sharing that cell with you. She knew about you and William's little secret, yet her mouth was closed to Paisley. She covered for you… Hmm, perhaps that's why she disappeared from Paisley's life", Willard's voice grows perturbed "Maybe the guilt of not doing what was right got the best of her! You see, that's the problem Serenity. No one does what's right anymore. No admission of fault, no stepping up to the plate and doing what is right by your so-called friend. Just sweep it under the rug, distance yourselves, and your hands are clean. Isn't that right?".

Serenity shamefully looks away as Willard stands up, pacing back and forth "But, not everyone sits back while bad things happen. Paisley stepped up to the plate. Jaxon stepped up to the plate".

"Who is Jaxon?" Serenity thinks.

"But you see, just because you hit the ball over the fence, doesn't mean you've hit a home run does it? Sometimes, it goes foul. I swear Jaxon has said that a million times" Willard digresses, shaking his head "Paisley and Jaxon may have saved me all those years ago, but they don't even remember. I'm no one to them, Serenity. No one. I thought I was important. But the next time I saw Paisley in the supermarket, well let's be honest, I stalked her and knew she'd be there. In any case, I smiled, and I waved. Do you know what she did?".

"Waved back?" Serenity answers sarcastically.

Willard angrily tosses his bottle of water across the room, closes his eyes, and takes a deep relaxing breath "That was rhetorical. But yes, she waved the gentlest, most I don't recognize you at all wave I'd ever seen. There was nothing indicating even the slightest recognition! And it has been that way ever since. For two years! And you know what? The same can be said for Jaxon! The two people who made me feel like someone for a night, took it all away. I killed William for Paisley. I killed Harvey for Jaxon. It was to protect them the way they protected me. And you know what? They will see me as a monster, no doubt. You know what my problem is? I blend in Serenity. That's what I do best, blend in, go unnoticed to the world. Who is Willard? Who cares right?".

"If you're so angry with them, why not just kill them? What does this have to do with me?" Serenity nonchalantly interrupts.

"Is it not clear Serenity? I… don't want them dead" Willard's mirthless laugh curdles Serenity's blood "I just want them… broken. I want them brought down to my level. Then and only then, will they truly see me. My two best friends will acknowledge me, and they will see why I had to do what I did. But to break them, I must hurt them. That humanity that Paisley holds so desperately near and dear to her heart, it'll be gone soon enough. She will be filled with so much anger, so much hate, that she'll have no choice but to murder someone she used to call friend. Your baffled expression tells me you have no clue. You, you're the friend Paisley will murder, Serenity. Try to keep up here, it's not rocket science. All it will take is losing Londyn and sending her proof of you and William's secret relationship. Whether you continue breathing or not, will be entirely up to her".

Serenity stands up, slowly approaching the locked cell that stands between her and Willard "She would never murder anyone. It's not in her nature to do that. You should be careful around her Willard. She has a deadly effect on people. If you value your life, you may want to live by your own advice. You know, step up to the plate and take responsibility for your actions. You're probably safer in prison".

Willard laughs bitterly "And there it is. That fire you have burning in your soul because I touched a nerve. You'd like to murder me, wouldn't you? Imagine what breaking a spirit will do. Imagine you've got nothing. Because that's what she will have. And Jaxon's hopeless romantic hero heart will follow right along with her. His anger and want for revenge against the person who hurt her, again you, will break him. He will be whispering murder in her ear. What do you think, when the police find your body, maybe they call us the murderous trio? Partners in murder? Is that too cliché?" Willard gives a dismissive wave, "Eh, we'll think of something".

"What if I could tell you where Chloe is? Would you let me go? She's the one you want anyways. If it wasn't for her, William would have never taken an interest in me. So, really, by your standards, Chloe is the problem, not me" Serenity negotiates.

A cold smile emerges on Willard's face "You really are the devious one, aren't you Serenity. Well, no time to think about that right now. I've got to run for coffee, it's almost eight o'clock. What's that place Londyn goes to every morning, Coffee Haven? Hmm, maybe I'll see her there".

"Hey, what about breakfast!? Something to drink!?" Serenity hollers as Willard walks away.

"I'll be back soon enough. Patience is a virtue, I hear" Willard climbs the dust filled wooden steps.

"You won't get away with this! You hear me!

You will be caught, you psycho!" Serenity yells angrily as she kicks the cot in her cell.

## Chapter Six

  Heavy-eyed and drowsy, Paisley wakes to the sound of crackling bacon paired with the aroma of freshly brewed coffee.

"Please tell me I did not fall asleep mid-sentence or something embarrassing" Paisley thinks rubbing her tired eyes, "just play it cool Paisley".

She subtly primps her curly hair, going for a less I-just-woke-up look. Paisley slowly moves to her side as she tucks her closed hand under her chin, getting a better view of Jaxon moving about his kitchen. She wears a soft, comforted smile as she watches him pour pancake batter onto a griddle. The fluffy pancake smell takes her back to her childhood. She would push a step stool as big as she was, climb up to kitchen counter height wearing a cheesy grin, and help her parents mix the pancake batter. She was an expert mixer; they would always tell her.

"Good morning" Jaxon's smiling, stubbled face greets Paisley as he flips a golden-brown pancake over.

"Good morning" Paisley's soft, husky voice responds, "I'm sorry I fell asleep here. I knew I was tired but didn't realize I was THAT tired".

Jaxon gives a dismissive wave "Oh, you're ok. It sucks not being able to sleep so, I'm just glad you were able to. Are you hungry?".

"I'm starving. Everything smells delicious" Paisley moves to a seated position on the couch, watching Jaxon transfer pancakes from the griddle to an oval serving platter.

"I hope you woke up with an appetite for a two. I tend to overdo it when I'm..." Jaxon pauses, but there's no stopping now, "trying to impress someone".

"Well, consider me impressed" Paisley smiles, raising from her seated position, surveying the dining table filled with golden scrambled eggs, crispy bacon, toasted bread, chopped fruit, and fresh squeezed orange juice.

Jaxon sets the silver-dollar pancake filled platter on the table and grabs the coffee kettle as he pulls Paisley's chair out "Coffee?".

"Yes please. Thank you" Paisley takes her seat feeling spoiled, "he's such a gentleman" she thinks as they begin eating breakfast together.

"So, um, last night, I was thinking about when we were at the bar and you mentioned how being around people makes you feel anxious, like you may be attacked. Have you ever thought about taking self-defense classes?" Jaxon chunks his pancake with his fork.

Paisley finishes crunching on her strip of bacon, her face flushes pink "You're going to think I'm ridiculous".

Jaxon scoffs, a curious smirk emerging "I'm sure I won't".

Paisley draws in a deep breath "About a year ago I convinced myself to go take some classes at this fighting gym. I expected there to be a lot of people like me; timid and looking for a way not to become a victim. And, I mean, maybe there was two or three that were. But the rest, I swear they were just there looking for an excuse to beat up on each other. I felt so out of place. Even the instructor was this intimidating, do it right the first time or I'm throwing you across the room type of guy. I never did go back after that first class. I don't know, maybe I went to the wrong gym? Or, maybe I'm just looking for a reason not to face my fears?".

"What if I taught you?" Jaxon's eyebrows raise.

"Oh, that's sweet of you but I couldn't ask you to do that. I mean, I... I'm sure I'll try again someday" Paisley's flimsy defense doesn't convince Jaxon.

"There's seven days in a week. Someday isn't one of them" Jaxon playfully reminds Paisley.

She crinkles her nose with a grin "Using my own advice against me? Clever".

Jaxon chuckles, a winning smile crosses his face.

"I guess I don't have anything to lose right? But would I have to hit you?" Paisley sips her orange juice, growing concerned.

"Eventually" Jaxon fills his spoon with fluffy eggs "I want you to be able to knock me clean out of my shoes by the time we're done".

"I've never known someone to be so excited to get knocked out" Paisley tucks a rogue curl behind her ear as she takes a bite of her maple syrup-soaked pancake.

Jaxon's laugh lights up his eyes. They continue conversing and digging into their breakfast.

Willard opens the door to Coffee Haven, his nostrils are immediately graced with the sweet smell of hot lattes and strong espressos. He scans the shop full of people and display stands intent on selling bags of ground coffee beans and little coffee shop novelties.

"There she is" he thinks taking sight of Londyn while he steps towards the front counter, joining the line of coffee deprived people, "same corner table, same book clasped between her fingertips, and the same cinnamon dusted, chocolate drizzled, frozen cappuccino".

"Welcome to Coffee Haven, can I interest you in a cold brew coffee or a chai latte?" A chipper, ruby-red haired barista asks.

Willard digs for his wallet, studying her name tag "You know Olive, I think a simple black coffee will do me just fine".

He wraps his hand around the coffee cup sleeve and makes his way towards Londyn.

She looks up from her book, feeling a cold aura as her light brown iris's connect with Willard's hollow, hooded eyes "That was creepy... And of course, he sits right behind me" she thinks, rolling her eyes as she shakes off the weird feeling and continues reading.

Staring at a colorful, decorated blackboard with the weeks specials and happenings, Willard loses himself in his head "Such a pretty face. It's a shame you'll be leaving us soon. No worries Londyn, I won't cut too deep. Unlike with William and Harvey, I actually don't want to murder you. But in any case, sometimes bad things must happen to good people" Willard takes a sip of his coffee, gripping the handle of his knife hidden in his jacket pocket "I hate to place any blame on Paisley, but it IS kind of her fault. If she wasn't so close to you, Londyn, maybe you'd make it through the mornings end".

Londyn's phone vibrates, a phone call from Paisley comes in "Hey girl! What's up?".

Paisley sits at her kitchen counter, crunching on the delicious apple chips she left Jaxon's apartment with "Oh my gosh! So, I have a lot to tell you. You should totally come over before you go to work today".

Paisley's cryptic response fills Londyn with curiosity "Talk about mysterious! Ok, give me like thirty minutes and I'll be over".

"Sounds good. I'm going to hop in the shower real quick" Paisley twists in her bar stool.

"Ok, never mind, give me like an hour, because girl, you take forever showers" Londyn laughs.

"What ever! I do not!" Paisley contends, "ok, maybe every now and then. Like seven out of ten showers? This is one of the three, I promise" Paisley giggles.

"Ok, ok. Forty-five minutes then" Londyn grins through the phone.

"Deal!" Paisley's upbeat voice gives Londyn a happy sigh as she hasn't heard Paisley so cheery in a long time.

Across the street, peering through the window of his squad car into the coffee shop is

Bishop.

He pieces together his thoughts as he grabs his cell phone to call Jaxon, watching an unsuspecting Willard.

Washing the dishes, Jaxon dries his hands on a kitchen towel and picks up his ringing cell phone "What's up Bishop?".

Bishop keeps his eyes on Willard, although it would be easier if the streets weren't full of hurried commuters "Hey man, I know it's early, but I need your help".

"Perfect timing. I was actually going to reach out to you today and tell you about a call Paisley and I received last night" Jaxon walks to his living room window, looking out at a sunshine day.

"Wait, I didn't realize you knew Paisley? That's the girl, the one who's fiancé was murdered. She's the one I interviewed" Bishop's expression puzzles.

"Yeah, I kinda put that together after the call we got from this dude. It's a small world and kinda crazy how we met. But that's a story for another day. Anyways, me and Paisley, we've been connected this whole time. This guy that murdered Harvey and her fiancé, he's targeting

US man. Some crazy shit, he feels like we betrayed him or something but, we don't even know or remember who he is" Jaxon places his palm against his cracked window.

"Damn. Well, I might be staring at him right now. Only thing is, I've got nothing solid so, I can't be for sure. And there's really not much I can do from here. There's this girl that went missing a few days ago, Serenity. I was just doing a routine door to door this morning and this guy; he gave me an unnerving feeling. Plus, he kinda pissed me off the way he called me officer instead of detective. I know it sounds petty, but he had an arrogance that most people who mistakenly call you the wrong title don't have. It was like he wanted to get under my skin. So, I followed my gut and trailed him to Coffee Haven, you know that little hipster coffee shop on 21st. Dude stands out like a sore thumb in there. Anyways, it could all be coincidence, but he sits behind this girl. I recognized her from that night Paisley's fiancé was murdered. She was Paisley's shoulder to cry on, Londyn. Not just that, but the girl who disappeared, she's friends with Paisley and Londyn too".

"Bro, that's gotta be him! You have to make sure he doesn't kill Londyn. That's Paisley's best friend. The last thing he said before he ended his message to Paisley and I was, keep your friends and family close. I'm sure he's not there to be social, he's there for murder" Jaxon's tone grows serious.

"I got my eyes on them, he ain't doing nothing with me here. What I was going to ask though is, I need someone to get into his house, quietly, while he's gone. If you know what I mean" Bishop wraps his palm around his steering wheel.

"Alright, yeah I'm picking up what you're putting down. Send me the address, I'll head out right now" Jaxon hurries to his room to get dressed.

"Will do. Oh hey, real quick. You have a chance to listen to that recording yet?" Bishop keeps his eyes on Willard.

"I did... I should've given you the chance to explain. When this is all over, we'll sit down and talk it over. For now though, I'm sorry that my temper and my ego got in the way of our friendship" Jaxon pulls a white t-shirt off its hanger.

"It's all good Jax. It was a messed-up situation. So, we cool?" Bishop grins.

"Yeah, we're good bro" Jaxon pulls a pair of blue jeans out of his busted wooden dresser.

The friends hang up, Bishop texts Willard's name and address to Jaxon.

Jaxon stares at the disheveled, off-white colored house "I don't even know what to expect when I get in there. Am I gonna find this missing girl? Dead bodies? A shrine to Paisley and I? TV murder mysteries don't exactly prepare you for the real-life shit".

Jaxon sneaks a look over his shoulders, ensuring there are no prying eyes as he creeps around to the backyard to find a less conspicuous entrance. He begins working the lock on the back door, the orchestral sound of bugs in the tall grass plays in the background.

The lock clicks "And we're in" Jaxon says proudly under his breath, stepping inside, quietly shutting the back door behind him.

"Damn, this place smells like death" Jaxon chokes, looking at a sink full of old dishes with crusted-on food.

His face sours at the sight of a garbage can overflowing with folded paper plates, crinkled up napkins, and crushed soda cans. Empty water bottles are scattered across the counter and floor, accented by greasy black banana peels and browned apple cores. Jaxon comes to a heavy-duty padlocked door. Tempted to yell out for the missing girl, he decides it best to scour the rest of the house to be sure he is alone.

Jaxon wears a curious look on his face as he enters a room with no door, a single pillow and blanket, and a cardboard box with a lid.

He approaches the box, pondering thoughts come to the surface "No furniture in any of the rooms, no decorations, nothing. Someone isn't planning on staying here very long".

Jaxon kneels and lifts the lid from the cardboard box. His brows crease together as he lifts a stack of photos out of the box. Jaxon scratches the back of his head, an uneasy feeling smacks the pit of his stomach as he scans the 5 x 7's plastered with Paisley's face. The park, grocery store, work, her apartment, lots of her in her apartment. Every picture tagged with a red, marker drawn heart around her face. Jaxon comes to pictures of himself. The number of pictures with his face severely outnumbered by the ones of Paisley.

Jaxon drops the photos at the sound of something hitting the window "Damn it!".

After a quick peak through the window that convinces him he's still alone, he returns to the box.

"Keepsakes?" He thinks shifting through the box "tickets to her performances, a sapphire gemstone necklace, a pink glove, receipts from her waiting on him, grocery lists? Really dude? My old wallet! And my i.d.! How did you even get this? And that was a pain in the ass to replace" Jaxon shakes his head, stopping his glance at the dropped pictures still scattered on the floor.

"Ahh and this must be you, Willard. So much for blending in. You really are a creep" He says aloud, picking up a picture Willard took of himself pretending to kiss Paisley, who was walking at the park in the background, "Alright, Bishop. We got our guy" Jaxon pulls his phone from his pocket.

Back at Coffee Haven, Londyn pushes herself away from the table, shoving her book down into her purse as she gathers her things to go and meet Paisley at her apartment.

"Leaving early are we?" Willard's brows furrow, "Hmm... well, it's showtime".

She passes Willard, a scent of expensive perfume wafts behind her. He gives a good, unsuspicious thirty seconds before he goes to follow.

His heartbeats quicken, ready for the next step in his plan to begin "Meet you at your favorite shortcut" he thinks, a devious smile plasters his face.

His smile quickly fades as he takes notice of Bishop's unmarked car, frustrated thoughts shove into his mind "They always think they blend in. Why do they think they blend in? I see you Detective Kent".

Willard watches Londyn disappear around the corner, completely unaware her life was just spared. He takes advantage of the busy sidewalks, ducking and weaving in and out of the crowds.

"Damnit, where'd he go?" Bishop loses Willard.

His phone goes off, Jaxon is calling.

"Hello Officer" Bishop looks up to see the brass knuckles right before they slam violently into his face, jerking his head to the side as he's knocked unconscious.

Willard grabs Bishop's cell phone and makes himself scarce.

Ten minutes of ringtone to voicemail, Jaxon begins snapping pictures of the contents in the box. He tucks some physical photos and the necklace in his pocket and approaches the locked door he can only assume houses the missing girl.

He focuses on the heavy-duty lock "There's no picking that. Only way in is break the lock or break the door"

Jaxon sets up to kick it down but is interrupted by shrill rings, "Finally! Bishop, we've got him! This guy is off the rails".

Willard's arrogant voice crackles through the phone "Ouch Jaxon, words cut like a knife you know".

"Where's Bishop?" Jaxon's veins fill with adrenaline.

"He's unavailable at the moment. And don't you

know not to go through things that are not yours?" Willard sits on an empty sidewalk bench.

"Where's the missing girl Willard!? Paisley's friend, Serenity, did you murder her? Or is she behind this door that's about to be broken off its hinges?" Jaxon's knuckles white around his phone.

"Oh Jaxon, I wouldn't do that. And Serenity? I would hardly call her Paisley's friend. You must have missed the pictures of Serenity and William cozying up while he was dating Paisley".

"I didn't miss the pathetic one you took of you with Paisley in the background" Jaxon jabs.

Willard's tone grows colder "It's not wise to poke the bear Jaxon. I'm not above killing at random to make a point. I must admit though, I underestimated you all. What's that you and your friends would say "caught me slipping?". I bet you think you're in a pretty good position right about now, am I correct?".

"Well, I'm not leaving here til you walk through this door. So, yeah, I'd say I do" Jaxon's confident tone makes Willard laugh mirthlessly.

"You've got to think outside the box, no pun intended. Do you really think someone like me wouldn't have a contingency plan in place, should things go awry? This safehouse means nothing to me. A mere stopping point on the journey home. In fact, the only thing I need from the dump in which you're standing, is my bargaining chip"

"The girl?" Jaxon grows annoyed.

Willard watches a couple holding hands walk by, "Precisely! Now, I know you Jaxon. So, I know you'd love to bust down that door and be the hero who saves Serenity. But if you were to do that, who saves Paisley when I break down her door, and replace Serenity with her?".

"You stay away from her! You hear me Willard!" Jaxon paces the room.

"Ah, I've touched a nerve. The hero's dilemma. Who will you save? Paisley sure does look beautiful this morning, doesn't she? Just look at her wearing the one thing she so often does not show; that innocent dimpled smile" From the bench, Willard admires an unsuspecting Paisley.

Jaxon grits his teeth as Willard continues "So, let me tell you how this plays out. You leave that house, I'll retrieve Serenity, and I shall not underestimate you again. And I would suggest you don't underestimate me either. Oh, and

Jaxon, NOTHING leaves that box! Now, if you agree, Paisley doesn't have to experience another traumatic event. Well, at least not yet. So, what do you say buddy? Do we have a deal?".

Through clenched fists and adrenaline filled veins, Jaxon agrees to Willard's terms, nearly throwing his phone across the room as Willard disconnects.

Paisley begins going through outfit choices for her evening performance at Mo's.

"Oh my gosh, I'm so happy for you Paisley! You let your heart open up, even if it was just the slightest crack. I mean, he made a full American breakfast for you!? AND homemade apple chips that you fell asleep on him making" Londyn giggles "Did The Jaxon Hotel come with a shirtless chef?".

Paisley blushes "Girl, you are too much".

"I cannot wait to meet him. Judging by the smile he put on your face, I think I'll like him" Londyn beams, happy tears glisten in her eyes before she replaces her smile with a serious glare "but I'll still cut him if he hurts you".

Paisley chuckles lightly "I'm not even sure what to make of it yet. All I know is, when I'm around him, I feel something I've never felt before, even with William... it's like this comfort encircles me and suddenly I'm not faking smiles and my heart has this constant giddy flutter, unless that's the heart murmur" Paisley bites the corner of her bottom lip, a pondering glance of her eyes "I find myself lost in his gaze. That sounds ridiculous though, right? I mean, aside from him helping me get my car unlocked the other day, we've spent one night getting to know each other, and suddenly I feel this fondness for him?".

Londyn side-eyes Paisley "First of all, you're so dramatic. The doctor said you do not have a heart murmur. Second, it's the flutter of infatuation. It's not ridiculous. Some people... when you connect, you just connect. Time doesn't matter Paisley, it's what you feel in your heart that matters".

"You should write for Hallmark" Paisley wears a frivolous grin.

"I'm serious Paisley" Londyn whines, trying to hold in her giggle.

"I know, I'm just..." Paisley takes a deep breath.

"Scared?" Londyn tilts her head.

Paisley sits on her bed "Yes. It's just... I feel myself letting go around him. And it scares me because... I know I'm not perfect. Far from it actually. This current version of me is sad. Oh my gosh, am I so aware of how pathetic I am" she rolls her eyes "I hate it. I crave to be me again; naïve and carefree" Paisley tilts her head towards the ceiling as if making a wish before locking eyes with Londyn "What if I'm not enough and all he sees is this broken girl. I feel so trapped in my own head. My anxiety tells me I'll never get better and this is just who I am, accept it. I swear I need a warning label "Immediately remove Paisley from your life if you experience the following side effects" she mocks.

"Girl, you are so much more than you give yourself credit for. Perfection is overrated and frankly, I don't think anyone is perfect. We all have our flaws, but they don't define us. You define who you are. You are the girl who stands up for people. You are brave. And behind those sweet, deep green eyes of yours, there is a fierce protector. And Jaxon, he obviously sees enough of that fierceness in you to offer self-defense lessons. How sweet is that!? Most guys are too macho for that. They'd rather you to sit back and let them be the hero. To me that says he doesn't see you as broken" Londyn wraps her friend in a hug.

Paisley smiles softly "You always know what to say... Now, if my heart does get broken again, you owe me so many boxes of Cookie Crunch! And I don't even want to hear it" Paisley's mouth playfully contempt.

Londyn fills the room with laughter "Deal! So, as much as I hate to change the subject, are you sure you don't want to go to the police about this serial killer stalker problem? I mean, the recording should be proof enough to do something, I would think" Londyn picks up a dress off Paisley's bed, "try this one".

Paisley inspects the dress before beginning to try it on "I don't know. I thought about it, but you remember how they reacted when I told them what I saw when William was murdered. I can picture them listening to this, whispering to each other with those stupid "she's psychotic" smirks on their faces and checking me in to a psych ward for creating a staged confession or something".

Londyn shrugs "The cute one that took your statement at least seemed concerned, like he wanted to help".

"Are you sure weren't just blinded by him and hoping he was" Paisley teases, a corner of her mouth quirks up.

"Maybe" Londyn scoffs nonchalantly, wearing a grin "That dress looks great on you by the way".

Paisley gives herself a once over in the mirror "Are you sure?".

"Girl! You look like you're dressed to go dreaming! Trust me, wear that" Londyn's playful tone grows excited.

Paisley tilts her head towards her shoulder, playfully over dramatic at the flattering compliment.

    Serenity wakes from a drugged slumber, taking a seated position on the dusty wooden floor of an old, spacious apartment.

Her eyes survey the decaying ceilings and walls, riddled with water damage just outside her new cell "What happened to the shithole I was in before this one?" she thinks.

Vague memories push themselves into her mind.

This wasn't the first time she'd been locked behind a door. She rests the back of her head against the wall. Being locked away, alone and hungry triggers the memories she'd buried so well, she almost forgot they existed. Growing up with an alcohol-addicted mother and an absent father was about as glamorous as it sounded. She thinks back on her middle school years when she'd be thrown into her room and locked away for hours, even days at a time while her mother would go on a binge. Serenity didn't dare make a sound for fear she would get the business end of the switch. So often, the alcohol would send her mother into a violent rage. And Serenity had the scars to prove it. By high school, she had grown defiant enough to fight back and run away.

Although she'd been putting on a brave face since Willard kidnapped her, her time in the cell, alone and hungry was beginning to break her. Although scary in his own way, he wasn't near as frightening as the monster behind her door years ago.

"In a strange way, it's almost as if you prepared me for this moment mother" she mutters to herself.

Her thoughts are shooed away as Willard finally returns with flimsy to-go boxes in his hands.

"And the prodigal kidnapper returns" she mocks, narrowing her eyes.

Willard sets his dark, brooding eyes on his captive "Oh good, you're awake. I was certain you were going to ruin my upholstery on the way here".

Serenity accepts the styrofoam takeout box containing a ribeye and a mountain of mashed potatoes, confused at Willard's statement.

He digs into his steak that could probably be heard mooing if the room was quiet enough "Do they come every night?".

"Willard, I'm starving and when I'm starving, you'll understand if I cannot think. You're going to have spell this out for me" Serenity's eyes roll to the back of her head.

"The nightmares. The ones that have you shaking, out of breath, and covered in cold sweat. The trembly whispers. The silent screams" Willard cocks his head to the side as Serenity grows uncomfortable "you know what I find curious? You whisper something to Paisley, every time you have the nightmare. Try as I might, I can never make out what you're saying. What is it you whisper to her?"

Serenity raises her shoulder in a half shrug, shoving mashed potatoes in her mouth as if she were in a competitive eating contest.

"Ok, I shall wallow in mystery for now" Willard drums his fingers on the worn-out dinner table.

## Chapter Seven

The sun begins its decent, rays of sunlight peeking through unoccupied spots between the tall buildings. Jaxon and Paisley walk the Belgian brick streets on the way to Mo's. Her text alert goes off as they approach the wrought iron handled, tall wooden door that looks more like an entrance to an exclusive club than a restaurant. The pair exchange silent glances as the alerts keep coming. Paisley covers her mouth with her hand, the other hand trembly swiping through pictures that may as well be daggers. For a moment, she forgets how to breathe. Her throat aches as she fights to hold back the flood behind her eyes.

Her weakened voice finds the ability to form

words again "What is this? This... I... this isn't real, it can't be?".

But she knows it is. She recognizes the little details that tell the story of a cheating boyfriend. The shirt she bought him for his birthday, being removed by a friend wearing a friendship bracelet that Paisley, Londyn, Serenity, and Chloe wore every day from Sophomore year to the day Paisley and Londyn bought new ones when Chloe and Serenity exited their lives. Paisley's heart squeezes, betrayal rings out like water in a soaked towel. It is replaced by a bitter cocktail of anger and sadness. Her eyes survey each picture. Serenity and William embrace like long lost lovers rekindling a flame. The treasured memories she had of William are chipped away until the very thought of him makes her stomach turn.

"How could you?" Paisley speaks under her breath to her ex-fiancé and friend; teardrops begin to trickle down her face.

Jaxon encircles Paisley in his arms, resting his chin atop her curly-haired head "I'm sorry you have to go through this. Betrayal cuts deep. The anger can take you to some dark places" he tilts her chin up, wipes her rosy, tear strewn cheeks, and gazes into her glistening emerald iris's "You will get through this. Willard is trying to break you".

"It feels like it's working" Paisley sniffles, pressing her face into Jaxon's shoulder, his shirt catching the tears that refuse to stay hidden.

Jaxon holds her close, his hand rests against the back of her head "You're stronger than he is Paisley. He doesn't think so, but I know you are".

A few hour-long minutes pass, Paisley begins to compose herself.

"What would Paisley Sinclair do?" A scoffing whisper to herself.

"Who?" Jaxon raises a brow.

Paisley blushes, realizing she whispered a little too loudly "Oh... sorry. My ass-kicking, billionaire alter-ego... I know I'm weird" she lets out a choked laugh, wiping her cheeks.

Jaxon smiles encouragingly "Come on, let's get you inside so you can crush your performance tonight" he wraps his arm around her shoulder, bringing her close.

Paisley leans her head on Jaxon's shoulder, followed by a comforted sigh.

Paisley takes in the smell of overly priced ribeyes and hickory smoked ribs. She passes beautifully stained, wooden tables decorated with expensive, colorful cocktails and fancy beer glasses. She navigates well-dressed servers and waitresses balancing trays cluttered with plates containing laughable portion sizes.

"I don't know how they justify paying so much for that. I guess if you have it, why not right?" she thinks, trying to keep her mind from wandering back to the pictures that tore at her heart moments ago.

Paisley takes her seat at the piano situated in a cozy back corner. She locks eyes with Jaxon and smiles softly as she sets to begin. She scans the restaurant, watching the groups of people in a state of bliss. Smiles fill the room. Eyes darting to her and back to whatever enthralling conversations are being had. She draws pointed fingers and some I-want-to-take-you-home looks. Paisley takes a deep breath and a sip of water from the glass delivered to her as she sat down. Paisley glances up, tucking a curl behind her ear.

Her heart sinks to the pit of her stomach, her

palms turn icy "it's him" she mutters as her vision tunnels and her pupils dilate "It's him!" She tries to yell but her voice won't cooperate.

Paisley's heartbeat quickens, her breaths struggle to keep up as she blinks her long lashes, trying to focus her eyes. Her eyes dart from table to table as Willard disappeared as quickly as he showed up.

Her head fills with harrowing images of Willard's dead eyes boring into her as William lay face down. She feels the walls of the restaurant closing in around her, the ache in her throat returning as she struggles to breathe. Voices of nearby diners' sound like distant echoes as she's seconds from passing out.

"Paisley? Are you ok?" Jaxon grabs hold of her, snapping her out of it.

"Our stalker. It was him. He was here. I recognized him from the pictures on your phone... he looked right at me with this... sickening grin" Paisley's head lowers, her voice shaky.

"Did you see where he went?" Jaxon glances over his shoulder, searching the restaurant with frantic eyes, hopeful he will get a chance to knock Willard on his ass.

"He was back there. And then he just disappeared" Paisley points, her face pale from the unexpected shock.

Jaxon cups the glass of water "I'm going to go after him. But first, drink some water and take some deep breaths. Everything is going to be alright".

Jaxon's voice coupled by the sincerity in his eyes sends a soothing feeling of safety through her body as her breaths return to normal.

"You still up for performing tonight?" Jaxon wears an encouraging quirk at the corner of his mouth.

"I think so, I won't let him win" Paisley throws on an apprehensively brave face.

"I'm sorry" she speaks into the microphone as Jaxon races across the marbled floor, to the back area where Willard stood a moment ago. Jaxon shoves the bathroom door open, a gentleman at the urinal turns in a confused gasp. Jaxon throws open each stall door; no sign of Willard.

"Where'd your little punk ass go Willard?" he thinks.

Jaxon follows the handsomely decorated hall to an unlocked door. On the other side, a dark, unoccupied party room. Jaxon pushes the door open, clenching his fist.

"There's nowhere to go Willard. Give it up already" Jaxon runs his unclenched palm against the wall, searching for the light switch.

He flips it on, Willard comes from the side, trying his hand at a brass-knuckled cheap shot, like the one Bishop received earlier. Jaxon ducks under Willard's fist and plants his knee into his rib cage. Willard is barely able to catch a winded cough before Jaxon's knuckles bruise his cheekbone. Jaxon sends Willard across a table, knocking chairs off their legs and centerpieces crashing to the floor. Willard tries, unsuccessfully, to get some leverage. Jaxon picks Willard up by his collar, shoving him against the wall and burying his forearm deep into Willard's esophagus.

"Your game is over Willard!" Jaxon pushes harder into Willard's neck.

Willard, mouth full of blood, can't hold back an ominous grin as he struggles to breath.

"You smile now, but you won't be when those bars slam shut behind you and your cell mate is bigger and badder than I am. How do you think you'll do in there huh?" Jaxon uses his free hand to grab his cell phone, ready to call Bishop to come arrest Willard.

"Paisley's going to overdose" Willard's emotionless voice can barely utter through Jaxon's forearms.

Jaxon loosens his grip, pushing off against Willard "What did you just say?".

Willard's giggle turns into a full-blown guffaw "You know, I always wondered how I'd fare in a fight with you, and well, I must say it went about as well as I'd expected" Willard spits out blood, trying to control his laughter as he digresses "You'll want to hang that phone up".

Jaxon screws up his face, reluctantly shoving the phone back in his pocket "What do you mean she's going to overdose? What did you do Willard!?".

Willard catches his breath, covering his rib cage with his busted hand, boastful chuckles creeping out "As always, I'm a step ahead. I imagine it must be absolutely deflating to be so close to taking me down, yet so far".

"You know, your "I'm-the-smartest-guy-in-the-room" routine is getting old" Jaxon glares at Willard.

"That doesn't make it untrue, my friend" Willard interrupts.

"I'm not your friend!" Jaxon fires back.

Willard meets Jaxon's fire, slamming his index finger on the table next to him "Oh I know you're not! And that is why we are where we are, now isn't it!? You and Paisley WILL be my friends just as soon as you give in and slip out of that sickening humanity! And what better way to make that happen than to force you both to live in paranoia. To know that I'll be lurking in the shadows. Watching... Waiting... Neither of you will ever truly be safe until you've embraced our friendship. Like right now for instance, Paisley did drink about half of her water, correct?" Willard scoffs "If only you'd known it was laced. I'd say right now, her heart is probably beating as fast as her sweet, overthinking mind".

Jaxon's eyes narrow, his brow creases.

"Ah, the worry in your eyes tells me you really care about her. Oh, don't worry, she'll have quite the trip. Kind of like the one Caroline had before you let her die on the bathroom floor. I wonder if Paisley will offer you the same innocent, save-me look Caroline did".

Jaxon's palms begin to sweat as he fights to

shove away fleeting memories of Caroline convulsing in his arms and the helpless feeling that clouded his mind. He never could wash away the guilt from that night. He tried, many times, to drown it in alcohol but the guilt was resilient.

"By all means Jaxon, keep me here and have me arrested" Willard presents his hands "But Paisley will suffer alone while we wait".

"Arrested? You know, you killed my brother, Willard. Maybe I just kill you and be done with it" Jaxon contemplates.

"And risk becoming as monstrous as me? Oh, I think not. I know you better than that. You know you better than that. You are a lot of things Jaxon, but a murderer you are not. Now Harvey on the other hand, he had murderous potential and he was dragging you down with him. I spared you from becoming him." Willard smooths his bunched-up collar.

"You didn't spare me from shit! Harvey wasn't perfect, neither am I. And if you think you can break me with murder, you really don't know me very well" Jaxon clenches his fists.

Willard leans against the wall "Oh I know violence isn't your weakness, Jaxon. Love is. You get it from your mother. At least that's what your sister says".

Jaxon grabs ahold of Willard's shirt, his knuckles turn white "You talk to my sister!?"

Willard raises his hands in defense "Woah, easy now. She's fine. I blend in, remember. People tell me stuff. It may be hard for you to believe, but I do have a moral compass. I would never take a mother from her child. I know what that's like. So, your dear sister and niece are safe. Paisley however, well you should hurry to her side, she's going to need you. Time and hydration are of the essence".

Jaxon's molars slam together "Why are you doing this to her!? Haven't you put her through enough? You're pathetic man. You really are. What made you so sensitive? You got your little feelings hurt because two drunk people in a bar who saved your ass from getting kicked, don't remember who you are? So, you go on this toddler tantrum, killing and ruining people's lives. It's all about to end, Willard. Sooner rather than later, you'll make a mistake".

Willard's blank stare through his hooded, dark circled eyes only further infuriates Jaxon.

Jaxon shakes his head, breathing a sharp, contempt breath. He pushes through the door and rushes to the main area of the softly lit restaurant.

"You can do this Jaxon. Please don't let her die tonight. He wouldn't kill her, would he?" he thinks, his hands shaking as he grabs a fresh water from the bartender.

He looks towards Paisley; struck by her aura as she serenades the diners.

The words sweetly escape her lips "To be only yours, I know now, you're my only hope".

Jaxon watches, frozen in place. The emotion in every word she sings, her eyes closed as she sways gently on the piano chair, she sends goosebumps throughout his entire body.

"I swear she's an angel" he whispers underneath his breath.

    As her song comes to an end, Jaxon navigates through the restaurant, trying not to make a scene "How are you feeling?" he asks.

"Much better than before. Did you find Willard?" Paisley reaches for her glass of water.

Jaxon stops her hand from bringing the glass to her lips "Here drink this one instead. Are you sure you're ok? You don't feel like you're going to pass out or anything? Rapid heartbeat, walls closing in, or something?".

Paisley smiles, giving a flattered giggle "I'm ok, Jaxon. Really, I am. Just seeing him freaked me out earlier. Maybe I was just seeing things?" she shrugs "What's going on? You seem worried".

Jaxon sighs, relieved "You know what, I'll tell you later. You're putting on a wonderful show. Willard isn't here. Just… let me know if you need anything" Jaxon takes up residence in a cozy booth near her performance area, watching closely for any changes in her demeanor.

## Chapter Eight

After a grand slam performance that filled her plastic tip jar to the brim, Paisley walks in the direction of Kent Gardens with Jaxon. A soft drizzle replaces the raindrops whose only evidence now are streetlight lit puddles and the smell of fresh rain in the air. Ambulance sirens echo in the distance, late-night commuters rush to their destinations.

"So, what's going on? You've been looking at me with cautious eyes all night. I know that look, trust me, I wear it all the time" Paisley scoffs lightly.

Jaxon wears a gentle smile before giving a defeated sigh "Willard... I had him. Right in my hands, beaten down, and ready to be arrested. But he used something from my past and played me like a fiddle. I should have known he was bluffing" Jaxon rubs the back of his neck, "he made me believe he drugged your drink and I was the only thing standing between keeping you alive or letting you die. I chose to let him go. I couldn't stomach taking a chance with your life. I hadn't felt that kind of fear since" Jaxon pauses, glancing across the street at graffitied storefront gates, "since my last girlfriend died of a drug overdose. I wasn't enough to save her. And I was sure history was about to repeat itself with you. I guess he knows I've got a soft spot for you".

"And... so do I" Paisley's gaze tiptoes to Jaxon's deep hazel eyes.

She shoves her curls back away from her face, her fluttering eyelashes send a warm tingle down Jaxon's spine "Can I say something crazy?".

"I think you've warranted as crazy a thought as you'd like" Jaxon grins, pushing the walk button on the crosswalk.

"Time to scare him away" she thinks, deciding to leap with faith, doing her best to ignore the nervous butterflies flying erratically in her stomach.

Paisley takes in a slow, deep breath "These past two years, I've watched the confidence I once had, slip away and turn into doubt. My bravery into apprehension. Friendships have dwindled. I hadn't even heard Serenity's name until I found out she was kidnapped. My anxiety has convinced me I'm broken, and that no one can handle me. It's been a lonely two years. I started believing that being alone for the rest of my life might not be so bad. At least I'd never get hurt, you know? Then you walked in and... you've awakened hope. I mean, I'm not saying I'm ready to spend the rest of my life with you like, right now. That would be crazy, I barely know you. But" Paisley squeezes her eyes shut "that didn't come out right. I don't mean I wouldn't want to spend my life with you. I meant... oh my gosh, I'm a mess. I really have a way with words, don't I?" Paisley slaps her palm to her forehead, her cheeks flush scarlet.

Jaxon laughs "No worries. I know what you're trying to say".

Paisley sighs, smiling bashfully as they walk down a London planetree lined street "I don't know, I guess, feeling my heart opening up at a time like this... it scares me. Either of us could be ripped away before we've ever been given the chance to get to know each other. He's trying to break us. What if he does?".

"The unknown can be nerve wracking, that's true. That unknown... it wants to keep us from living life. It lies to us. Telling us to live in fear of it, so that we never find out what's on the other side. I get that, more than you know. Losing my girlfriend to a drug overdose changed me, probably worse than what losing my brother did. Maybe because after losing Harvey, I just sunk back to the familiarity of anger and alcohol. I shielded my heart and deflected anything that looked like it had the potential to blossom. I guess I've been afraid to care again. I don't know. It's like, I know what the unknown is doing but I don't stop it. I just open another bottle, fight for my next two-grand, and tell myself I'll deal with it another day. And then another day comes. And another day" Jaxon scoffs, looking towards the sidewalk.

"Oh Jaxon, we really are beautifully broken, aren't we?" Paisley inspects her fingernails.

Jaxon slows to a stop, wrapping his palm gently around Paisley's arm. The gesture delivers a soft gasp and an enchanting tingle throughout her body.

Jaxon studies her innocent gaze, noticing the voluptuous pout of her lips and her defined cupid's bow "Nah... you're just beautiful Paisley. And for the first time in a long time, I want to know what's on the other side of unknown".

"So do I" Paisley can barely mumble the words as her heart fills with giddiness.

Her body gravitates to Jaxon's. She's not sure if he pulled her in or the universe pushed them together. A haze of tantalizing perfume and cologne surrounds them. The streets never seemed so quiet. Paisley runs her soft hand across Jaxon's rugged face, wrapping her arms around the back of his neck. Their lips so close, she's sure he can taste the Zinfandel she had after her performance. Her doe-eyes ask him to be good to her. His strong, gentle hand embracing the small of her back, is a resounding assurance he will. Paisley's heartbeats continue to race. She can't feel herself breathing. Jaxon brushes a loose curl from her face, tucking it behind her ear. A light breeze glides through the heat between them as Jaxon leans in, caressing Paisley's lips with his, un-cluttering the mess that is each of their lives. If even just for a moment, the anxiety, the fear, the anger vanishes. She closes her eyes and tightens her grasp around his neck. Each hug of their lips grows sweeter, more powerful. The crumbling walls around their hearts stand no chance of holding up any longer.

For a moment, they stop, pressing their foreheads softly together, gazing deep into one another's eyes. Jaxon steals Paisley's breath as he caresses her Zinfandel flavored lips once more.

He pulls softly away, staring at Paisley staring at him.

"Let's summon Paisley Sinclair tonight" Paisley's eyes glimmer under a dim streetlight.

Jaxon tilts his head "What do you mean?".

"I'm tired of being afraid... Let's train tonight" Paisley gently draws the corner of her bottom lip between her teeth.

Jaxon smiles at the spark he knew she had inside coming alive "Ok, let's do it".

A sporty ponytail, workout pants, and a sports bra are all it takes to bring Paisley Sinclair to the forefront of Paisley's being. Sweat drips down Paisley's stomach and the small of her back, flashbacks come and go with every strike she lands. The fire that took her parents. The face of the man who took her unfaithful fiancé. The friend who smiled in her face, lying as she slept with William. Sadly, even William's face, who she'd mourned for so long, graces the stitched leather. Jaxon watches on as Paisley, the fainthearted, curly haired blonde works her confidence back up. She breathes heavily as her arms are all punched out.

Paisley wipes the sweat from her beaded brow, grabs a water bottle from the glass end table and chugs it "That felt really good. Oh my gosh, I didn't realize how much I needed that".

"It's definitely a stress reliever. And not as frowned upon as delivering your knuckles to someone's face in the back of an alley" Jaxon steadies the punching bag, relieved she wasn't scared away when he told her about his illegal way of making a living.

Paisley giggles, interlocking her fingers behind her head, her breath returning "so, have you always had a winning relationship with fighting?".

Jaxon threads a hand through his hair "Oh no. I've had my share of losing. I remember when I got in my first fight, my mom was pissed. She was standing there in the entryway to the kitchen, arms crossed over her flour covered apron, tapping her foot on the ground, drilling me with questions. I couldn't read my dad though. He just sat at the dining table, looking over the top of his newspaper at my busted face. He had this stern, intimidating look. After a moment, he just asked "Did you win?". I told him it was two people against one. It wasn't a fair fight. He closed his newspaper, set it down and I winced, ready for another ass whooping. Instead, he gave me an inspirational speech "Fair? Life ain't fair Jackie. It's a street fight, you do what you gotta do to win. That's the way life is. We do what we gotta do to survive". The same kids jumped me again the next day".

"And you won this time?" Paisley sits on the wooden floor, sets her water bottle beside her, and leans back on her palms.

Jaxon laughs "Nah, I still got my ass kicked. But I left one of the kids with a cut deep enough they didn't find it fun to mess with me anymore. I suppose that's kind of a win, right?" he lifts his shoulder in a shrug.

Paisley giggles, nodding in approval "Oh! Hey, so Londyn said she'll be able to make it over tomorrow afternoon. Did your sister and niece get out of town safely?".

Jaxon takes a seat next to Paisley, his legs sprawled out in front of him "Yes they did. Freya is over the moon because the hotel has a pool. I hate that they had to go, but I know it's the safest thing until we take Willard down".

Paisley takes a sip of water "That's for sure. With all of us putting our heads together, we have to be able to think of something to get a step ahead of him. The last thing I want is the paranoia he promised. He really is insane, isn't he?".

"No question about that" Jaxon rubs his hands together.

Paisley curls her knees to her chest and leans her head onto Jaxon's shoulder "I hope we get to him before he hurts anyone else" she says softly.

"Me too" Jaxon wraps his arm around Paisley, repeating his sentence in his head "Me too".


Willard returns to Serenity's new home. He slams the light switch up as he struggles dragging a body bag across the floor.

Serenity startles, rising to her feet, her back against the wall.

Her reaction causes her to knock her cup of water

over "Shit! What... who is that!?".

Willard slowly turns his head in Serenity's direction, his eyes looking right through her "You'll excuse me while I conduct some unfinished business".

Serenity watches as he unzips the body bag, flipping the body over "Chloe!" Her voice weakens "is she... dead?".

"Oh, she's very much alive... For now" Willard sets an unconscious Chloe in a seated position against the wall.

Chloe's head falls, slumping her over. Willard pushes her back up, grabbing a butcher's knife from inside the end table next to her.

Serenity approaches the edge of her cell closest to Willard "So can I go now? You've got Chloe, you don't need me anymore" Serenity's skin crawls, panic slowly setting in "Right?... Willard?" She backs away, tripping over the afternoon's empty to-go box as he rises to his feet and looks over his shoulder.

A muffled laugh beneath the mask he's now wearing tells her she's going nowhere "Oh my dear Serenity. You look at me with those innocent eyes. I'd almost believe it; you don't look like a murderer. But then again, I suppose without this mask, I don't either. But you are, aren't you? Oh, believe me, the irony is not lost upon me. A murderer kidnapping a murderer".

"No, I'm not! I'm not a killer like you!" Serenity's eyes fill with tears of anger.

"I'm sorry mom, stay with me! I'm so sorry" Willard mocks "Those words tremble away from your beautiful lips every night before you shake yourself awake, whispering what I can only assume are endearing words to Paisley. Does she know you killed your mother? Did she help you do it? Maybe her putting a bullet in you isn't so farfetched after all" Willard's hands pull him from cell bar to cell bar, taunting Serenity.

"Get away from me!" Serenity cowers into a ball, the flashbacks she tucked away of the beatings she endured when her mother was out of her mind, flood back into her skull.

Willard lets out a grim chuckle, turning his attention back to Chloe, leaving Serenity in her panicked state.

Willard stares at Chloe, passed out "Time to wake up".

He inspects his butcher's knife, running his

finger up the blade and pricking it at the top. He plasters a menacing smile beneath his mask as a single strand of blood trickles down. He bends to Chloe's level and takes hold of a chunk of hair to hold her head up. He digs the knife into her face, slicing her from jaw to ear. Chloe wakes to the coarse of pain.

Willard covers her scream, her blood drips over his fingers "Do try to be quiet dear. No one can hear you up here and my ears tend to be a bit sensitive".

Chloe's eyes widen, her pupils dilate as her palms begin to sweat.

Willard loosens his hand from her mouth, a blood-curdling scream releases from Chloe's lungs, desperately calling for help.

Willard winces, clenching his jaw as the decibels remind him of his strict grandmother yelling at him before she gave him the beatings she so loved to hand out.

"The hard way it is" he cuts a piece of duct tape and slaps it across Chloe's mouth.

Willard stands by the living room window, peering into the night. He grabs his cell phone and begins a video call to Jaxon.

Jaxon stares at his screen, still cuddling Paisley in his arms. They exchange silent glances before he answers, "Why don't you quit with this mysterious bullshit, Willard".

"Ah come on, but it's so much fun to watch you squirm. Where's Paisley? Did she make a full recovery?" Willard bursts into taunting laughter before pulling himself back together "Oh come on Jaxon. You couldn't even save Caroline. Do you think I would really risk my most prized possession, given your track record?".

Jaxon's brows draw together "You stay talking a lot of shit in a safe place. But I bet you're real quiet when you're not. How's your face by the way?".

"Much better than our special guest here" Willard's voice grows serious, he focuses the camera on a disoriented Chloe, dried blood staining her cheek.

"That's Chloe" Paisley whispers under her breath, clutching her stomach, feeling like she may throw up.

"I'm going to put on a show here soon. Though,

undoubtedly, not quite as interesting as the one Serenity put on with William, but what can you do? The pictures, Paisley. Did you enjoy them? I didn't either" Willard answers his own question "It pained me to send them to you. After all, you are my best friend. But best friends must share the hard truth and the truth is, Chloe and Serenity were not your friends Paisley. Serenity slept with William as you lied on the couch, watching movies and crunching on candy and popcorn, waiting for him to come back home. Chloe knew about their late nights together, yet she never said a word to you".

"Just let them go Willard! I don't care what they did! What's done is done" Paisley pleads.

Willard sets the phone on a tripod facing Chloe "Oh, I know you don't mean that" Willard runs the knife across Chloe's neck, using it to brush a strand of silky black hair away from her face "Come on, tell me you don't want to kill one of them for the bitter betrayal?".

Willard turns his masked face towards the camera. Paisley gasps, blinking away terrified memories of the night in the park.

Willard shakes his head "Look at you. The mask you remember, but me, you never remembered me. Fascinating how the mind works. How memories work. It's almost as if we're powerless to keep the memories we want. We get what we get, and we don't throw a fit. Try as I might, my grandmother's attempt at life lessons will just will not leave my head. In any case, Chloe or Serenity, which life do I take, and which one will you take?".

"That's not the way the world works Willard. You don't kill people just because they've wronged you!" Paisley grows frantic.

"Oh, little dove, aren't you the virtuous one. Well, just because you are delusional doesn't mean I have to be. Chloe it is!" Willard looms closer to Chloe, his knuckles white around the grip of his knife.

Paisley's hands cover her mouth, she gasps as Willard sticks the knife deep into Chloe's stomach and exits from view of the camera. Chloe fights for her last breaths, blood fills her mouth, dripping down her chin. She coughs up blood, her eyes go blank as she slumps against the end table. Serenity's screams push through the phone.

"Look what you've done Paisley!" Serenity yells "You and your BLEEDING HEART! You saved THIS monster? We were wrong! It doesn't just get YOU in trouble. It gets everyone around you

DEAD! You are dangerous Paisley! You hear me! It's your fault Chloe is dead. It's your fault William is dead. My mother would still be alive if it wasn't for YOU and LONDYN! Even your parents would probably still be ali".

Jaxon hangs up the phone, cutting her off.

Paisley slowly steps towards Jaxon's couch, takes her seat, rests her elbows on her knees, and buries her face between her palms. Jaxon sits next to her and takes her in his arms.

"Am I a bad person?" Paisley stares at the scuffed wooden floor.

"No, you're not a bad person" Jaxon lifts her chin up "hey, none of that is on you. Willard and his warped way of trying to earn our friendship created the situation we are all in right now. Him and him alone".

Paisley sighs, turning her face away "It's weird. I feel like I'm supposed to be devasted, but… if anything, I'm just angry. How does she have the nerve to attack me after what she did? Like she wasn't sleeping with William behind my back. And her mother? Serenity hated her mother. She was an alcoholic and was mean… so mean. She used to lock Serenity in her room for days, throw stuff at her if she didn't move fast enough, and beat her whatever reason she decided fit for the day. Serenity used to tell us that one day she would kill her for what she put her through. Of course, we didn't take her seriously because she only ever mentioned it when she was really wasted. And she'd laugh afterwards. But when her mother did die, it was always... suspicious to me".

"Suspicious?" Jaxon's expression grows curious.

Paisley picks at her fingernails "The night before, me and the girls went out. This was maybe a few weeks before William was murdered. In fact, remember that singing competition I told you I entered and won?"

Jaxon nods, rubbing his palm across his jawline.

"Well, this was the night I found out my friends secretly signed me up for it. Anyways, so Londyn and I went to pick Serenity up from her mom's house, which was weird because Serenity was staying with another friend at the time. She hadn't lived at home in years, but she told us her mother was sober now and wanted to talk, so just pick her up there. We assumed they were going to mend things. It was clear pretty quickly that was not the case. Londyn and I walked in, the house was overrun with empty liquor bottles, beer cans, and just, trash. We heard a commotion in one of the rooms. Serenity was standing over her mother with a liquor bottle raised up and ready to come down on her mother's head. We were shocked, so was Serenity when she saw us. She told us to leave and wait in the car so, reluctantly we did. When Serenity came out ten minutes later, she told us she just needed to confront her mother about the way she treated her, nothing else happened, and that was the last she wanted to speak of it. Her tone and the look on her face, it wasn't the Serenity I knew. Then again" Paisley sighs "that girl mastered the art of deception. I don't know, maybe I never really knew her like I thought I did. But the next day we found out her mother died when she drunkenly tripped over herself and hit her head on the corner of a table. At least, that was Serenity's story before she started to distance herself from us. I never understood why the cops didn't seem to really investigate her death as suspicious. I guess, maybe they didn't question it because they had been called out to her house so many times for drunk and disorderly conduct. More like, completely wasted and disorderly".

"Sounds like there's more to her story than what she let on" Jaxon leans back on the couch cushion.

Paisley rubs her hands on her thighs "I think so

too. Makes me wonder if she could have made good on her threats against her mother. I mean, if her mother tripped and fell, what would that have to do with me and Londyn?".

"Exactly. I guess you never know how much you really know someone. Growing up, my brother used to tell me, we all have a face we show to the world and a face we keep to ourselves. And if you're lucky, one day you'll be able to share the face you keep to yourself with someone else and they won't totally hate you for it. I never really understood what he meant when he said that. He was always trying to be philosophical… and he failed most of the time" Jaxon scoffs gently "but when I started dating Caroline, the girlfriend that died in my arms, I began to understand what he meant. I wasn't into drugs like she was. You'd have never guessed she was struggling with addiction. Her smile was radiant. She was very positive. Addiction wasn't new to me though. I'd seen it before. Shit, I'd had my own struggles with alcohol that was borderline addiction, or maybe it was? I'm not really sure when it goes from an unhealthy coping mechanism to addiction. Anyways, watching someone I cared for so deeply, struggle, that was new, and I hated it. So, I decided I'd go cold turkey and get sober. Cold turkey wasn't an option for Caroline though. She was in too deep and she needed help. It took some convincing, but she finally agreed to enter treatment. The day before her first day of treatment, we were supposed to celebrate with virgin margarita's and homemade chocolate chip cookies. Instead, it ended with my tears hitting her chest as she convulsed in my arms. She wanted a farewell high, and it killed her. I felt like I should have known. I should have seen what she was planning" Jaxon lowers his head.

"You couldn't have known. Some people are just better at hiding their struggles" Paisley rubs his shoulder.

## Chapter Nine

*One year ago*

Paisley fidgets in the plastic chair that was obviously not meant for comfort, as her turn to share arrives. She makes passing glances at the circle of unfamiliar eyes.

"Am I really going to do this" she thinks.

Paisley draws in a long breath "Hi, my name is Paisley".

"Hi Paisley" the support group responds in unison.

"Umm, I'm not really sure how this works" she laughs nervously, hooking her ankles around the legs of the chair.

"Just tell us whatever you'd like to tell us. Whatever you feel comfortable sharing. Perhaps when you first noticed the feelings" the group leader, Samantha, smiles politely.

Paisley chews at a fingernail "Ok... Umm, I guess my anxiety really took over after my ex-fiancé was murdered. I..." She pauses, continuing after a nod of encouragement from Samantha "I just remember standing there, alone in my head. My heart rate quickened and my throat dried while I watched the life leave his eyes. I could see my chest rise and fall but I couldn't feel myself breathing. My stomach was numb, so were my arms. Everything, but the killer's eyes on me, distorted. The sounds of the night echoed around me. With the knife still grasped in his hands, I knew I was next. I told myself to run, but I couldn't. Or maybe I just didn't want to. Instead, I stood there, frozen with fear, pleading silently "if you're going to kill me, please make it quick". But he didn't. He just stared at me for what felt like hours and then disappeared. I was so in shock I don't even remember when the police got there. When I was finally able to answer their questions, I tried explaining what I'd seen. They seemed dumbfounded and more interested in me answering their accusatory questions. "Was my fiancé abusive? Was he cheating? Did I hire someone to kill him? Had we argued recently? Of course, we argued, what couple doesn't? It wasn't a robbery and I was untouched. I guess it looked too random for them to believe. I started to feel like I was guilty. That's crazy. Here I was, a victim, and I felt like maybe I had done something wrong. Maybe there was something I could have done. Was it my fault? On top of that, they never found the killer.

*Present day*

Paisley tosses and turns under her blankets. She jerks her head from side to side trying to escape the nightmare unfolding.

*"Paisley, where'd you go?" The woman's hollow voice echoes.*

*Paisley draws in ragged breaths; her eyes study the lone strip of light peeking through the bottom of her door.*

*Chains scrape across the floor as the woman continues her search "Come back here Paisley. Come back where it's safe".*

*The chains continue to follow the woman's voice*

*until, like a storm that changed its course, there is nothing. Paisley narrows her eyes, leaning her ear unwillingly towards the door as she no longer hears the rattling chains, nor the ominous voice.*

*The door handle rattles violently, Paisley flinches back, falling on her elbows as the voice returns, angrier "PAISLEY! You can't hide forever! You're not safe out there! Think of all the bad stuff that could happen if you don't come back!".*

*"Go away! You're not real! Please! Just leave me alone!" Paisley pleads, tears in her voice "I don't want to be in there anymore".*

*"People around you don't DIE when you're in here, Paisley" the woman negotiates.*

*"No... but I do" Tears make their descent from the corner of Paisley's eyes to the middle of her cheeks.*

*She presses herself up against a wall, doing her best to keep the tears off her face. The door swings open, a curly haired silhouette stands in the doorway, chains hanging from both arms.*

*"Better you than someone else" the woman fast approaches.*

*"I can't live like this anymore!" Paisley*

*screams.*

She shoots up in her bed, hyperventilating. Her trembling palm quickly wipes a lone tear away. She grabs her phone off the nightstand and falls back onto her pillow, wrapping herself in the blanket to fight the cold breeze from a window she forgot to close before she went to bed.

The slam of a car door sends her phone out of her hands "Damnit" she mumbles.

Paisley slides out of bed and approaches the window with the intent of shutting it. Instead, she opts to sit at the window bench and watch the cute couple who probably just got home from a night out. She brings her knees to her chest; a soft smile graces her face. The smile slowly disappears. She looks away and focuses on the nail polish that's begun to chip away from her toes as thoughts of William enter her mind. She moves her eyes back to the window, staring off into the distance, lost in what are now ruined memories.

"What did I do wrong William?" she thinks, "When did you fall out of love with me? I was faithful, we laughed, we cried. You asked me to marry you. Why? Why Serenity? She was the wild one, you hated that about her. You always said you didn't trust her. I suppose I'll never know".

A fleeting memory surfaces of her mother's advice after her first break-up.

*She'd locked herself in her room, the world was over. Of course, it wasn't, but that's what it felt like. When her mother convinced her to open the door, she sat next to her with comforting words "Sweetie, one day, you'll find a man who doesn't just make you smile from ear to ear. He will make you mad, he will make you cry, and even make you want to tear your own hair out. But at the end of the day, if that man holds you gently, kisses you sweetly, and fills your heart with happiness, you know you've found him. The ones who break your heart along the way are just pointing you towards the one who will cherish your beautiful soul. Most importantly, my sweet girl, always remember that happiness comes from within. Don't look to someone else to give it to you".*

Paisley focuses back on the couple kissing goodbye. She places her palm against the side of her neck thinking about the kiss her and Jaxon shared earlier. His lips pressed against hers, her body against his. She had no words to describe the feeling, only a dimpled smile and a warm comfort as sweet as the apple pie her mother used to make. Paisley unlocks her phone, scrolls her contacts, and stares at Jaxon's name.

Across the way, in a vacant building where Serenity sleeps on a worn wooden floor, Willard watches Paisley from the window "I wonder what you're thinking about. Your smile is truly fascinating. It's a shame you don't bring it out more often. Soon, my lovely woman, I'll give you a smile that never fades. Everything I do for you is out of love. You'll understand someday, I just know you will. And if you don't... well... you will".

Back at Kent Gardens, Jaxon stands at his kitchen counter; a bottle of cheap whiskey in his palm, a whiskey tumbler in his other hand. He spaces out as he sets to pour.

"I'm sorry I couldn't save you Caroline. We almost made it" he thinks, staring out his window at a picturesque scene of lit up city buildings.

Jaxon glances at his phone, a text comes through

from Paisley.

He sets the whiskey tumbler in a puddle of leaky sink water and picks up his phone to read Paisley's text "I could really use some company".

Jaxon puts on a smile. He thinks about the moment they shared. Her soft lips between his, the way his heart let go and accepted hers. If he had to describe what he felt in that moment, words could never do it justice.

Jaxon tips the whiskey bottle over, pours it into his sink, and flips the water faucet on to drain the alcohol "I don't need you anymore" he thinks.

He swipes his screen to start a text to Paisley "I could too. Meet you at your place in ten minutes?".

"I'll be here waiting" Paisley's text reads.


Willard's face puzzles as Paisley leaves her position at the window bench, making her way from her bedroom to the living room. He watches her approach her front door. He can't hold back a smile, as she takes a quick second to make an adjustment to her hair and tugs at the bottom of her shirt to smooth it down. When she opens the door, jealousy floods Willard's heart as Paisley's arms wrap around Jaxon, his around her.

Willard slams his back against the cracked wall beside the window, squeezing his eyes shut and taking in a harsh breath "It's just a friendly hug Willard, no need to worry. She's your girl, Jaxon stands no chance. He didn't save her, you did! You know what, let's not watch them right now. No telling what pathetic attempts we'll see. Now, where's that bottle of wine".

Willard finishes the last drip of a strong Cabernet "Ok forget it, what are they up to".

"The lights! Why are they off!?" Willard's blood boils, his mouth sets in a hard line as the vein pops out of his neck "Paisley, you seductress! I hadn't pegged you for a girl who'd be sharing her bed already! That's it. Tomorrow… you break!".

Paisley stands against the concrete ledge

"I've never been up here before. I would have never guessed there was a view this stunning right above us".

Jaxon smiles, standing next to her with his arm around her waist "It really is. I know it's kind of cliché".

"Kind of?" Paisley grins mischievously, the gentle breeze plays with her hair.

"Ok, a lot cliché" Jaxon scoffs lightly "but as long as security doesn't catch you up here, it really is peaceful. In a big city kind of way. It's like you get the sounds of the city and the stillness of the night all at once".

"I would never have guessed you liked the sound of silence" Paisley's eyes gleam under the moonlight.

Jaxon chuckles "If you would've grown up in my house, you would pay for the silence. I didn't even know it existed until I moved out. Imagine my surprise when I heard it for the first time".

Paisley cracks up with laughter.

She composes herself, looking up into Jaxon's eyes "Have you ever had anyone up here before?".

"You're the first" a corner of Jaxon's mouth quirks up.

"Well, I feel pretty special to be sharing your secret spot with you" her heart flutters as she turns her face from his, back to the cityscape.

"Do you ever dream about going to back to Georgia and leaving the city life behind?" Jaxon's voice fills with wonder.

"I do. I mean, I'm afraid I'm more New Yorker than small town girl now, but a simple life sipping wine on the back porch, recording songs in a little basement studio, doing local performances, nothing grand you know? That sounds like a perfect life to me" Paisley turns and faces Jaxon "What about you? What does your perfect life look like?".

Jaxon watches her curious eyes before he looks out over the city "I've never been outside of the five boroughs, but I've always dreamed of being a famous artist. I would have a mansion with so many rooms I'd get lost and just pick one to sleep in, acres of land, fancy parties like the movies. I know, it probably sounds ridiculous" Jaxon laughs, raking his fingers through his hair.

"Hey, that's not ridiculous. That's your dream. It can happen" Paisley wraps her arms around his

"Just promise you won't forget me when you're a rich artist sipping fifty-year-old scotch in your Great Room" she tries her hand at a fancy accent.

Jaxon grins, giving her a playful push "How could I forget you if you're coming with me? You know, there IS a girl in my dream too".

"Oh, there is?" Paisley wears a playfully intrigued look "Let me guess, she's like a supermodel with big boobs and legs for miles?" she giggles.

Jaxon places his hands on either side of her hips and faces her "Well... if I'm lucky, she has long, curly blonde hair. Deep emerald eyes that you could spend all day in. A laugh that wrinkles her nose. She smells like cotton candy and has a smile that she tries to hide but her cute dimples show up anyways".

Paisley feels a flush creeping up her face as she smiles, twisting a curl around her finger "You're kind of crazy, you know that?".

"Why's that?" Jaxon brushes a strand of Paisley's hair from her face.

Paisley lowers her head, studying the area they stand in "You've already got a lot going on in your life and here I come waltzing in to complicate it more. I'm like a storm and yet, you're not running away".

Jaxon tilts her chin up and presses his lips against hers "You're a storm worth chasing".

She wraps her arms around Jaxon's neck, her eyes glistening "I'm going to annoy you so much one day" she lets out a choked laugh.

Jaxon scoffs gently "And I'm going to frustrate the shit out of you someday".

Paisley giggles, wiping happy tears away from her eyes "I'd love that".

"I would too" Jaxon kisses her forehead and wraps her in his arms.

## Chapter Ten

A fresh morning arrives, sunshine reflects off the resilient puddles that have yet to evaporate from last evenings rain.

Serenity wakes to Willard staring "Has anyone ever told you, you have an annoying smile?".

"Someone woke up on the wrong side of the floor" Willard laughs obnoxiously, trapesing across the room to grab a plate full of slightly burnt peanut butter toast and a juicy ham slice "I just... try as I might, I cannot make out what you mumble before you wake. You absolutely must tell me before Paisley kills you".

Serenity rolls her eyes, moving to a cross-legged position "So, if I'm going to die, do I ever get to know anything about you? You owe me something. I piss in a bucket, I haven't showered since you kidnapped me, I barely eat. Humor me, Willard. Who are you?".

Willard takes a seat on an old leather armchair across Serenity's cell, digging into his food "I thought you'd never ask. Well, let's see, I was born at Brooklyn State Hospital. I was 7 pounds... I'm kidding of course. Who wants those boring details? You want the juicy stuff. How did I become a selfless do gooder who saves people that don't give a shit about me, am I right?".

"Selfless do gooder?" Serenity scoffs.

Willard grins "Well when I was five years old my father threw a temper tantrum and murdered my mother. He was killed in a standoff with police and I was sent to live with my sweet, loving grandmother. Again, kidding. She was about as sweet as the pickled eggs she thought she so masterfully made. My father inhcrited her temper. If you'd like proof, I can take my shirt off and"

"Umm, no I'm good. I'll take your word for it" Serenity interrupts, tossing her hair to the side.

"Suit yourself" Willard straightens his posture.

"So, you had a screwed-up family and in turn now you're screwed-up? How original. Join the club" Serenity checks her empty cup, hoping water still sits inside.

Willard chuckles "Oh, no my dear, I only tell you that as a premise for why home was never really home. No, for me, home was a park bench, a cafe seat, a sidewalk bench, wherever I could just sit and watch and listen. For hours, my ears would take it all in. People disappointing each other. Spouses apologizing for their unfaithfulness. Brothers and sisters fighting, not forgiving. Friends spilling secrets for the sake of cheap entertainment. I grew tired of watching people. Over the years, the more I observed, the more I found myself wanting to stop people from breathing. So, I no longer wanted to watch. But I had zero friends. Literally, it was like I didn't even exist. Until one fateful day, when I entered a bar I had no business being in and was handed the most attention I'd had since the last time I received the paddle to my ass. After Paisley and Jaxon saved me from a group of guys who obviously had masculinity issues, I decided I'd watch them. After all, maybe following two people's lives wouldn't be quite as gut wrenching as the consistent bullshit I heard from all the randoms".

"So, you decided becoming a stalker was better than being an eavesdropper?" Serenity wears a baffled expression.

"Stalker? No, I'm not a stalker, Serenity. I lived vicariously through each of them. Jaxon was the cool, tough guy I wasn't. Paisley was the gorgeous girlfriend I'd never have. I especially enjoyed watching her. But I soon realized, watching them was no better. I suppose I could admit it was actually worse. I got to know the people in their lives; the ones they loved, the ones they hated, the ones that hurt them. I saw their dreams and ambitions going down the drain. Their lives were falling apart, and they couldn't even see it. Each needed saving, the way they saved me. Paisley was first, poor girl. Cooking meals for a boyfriend who had no intention of showing up until late at night. Cleaning a house that he'd never notice even needed it. Falling asleep waiting on an uncomfortable couch. She was naïve, and he knew it. I suppose that's why he was so good at replacing her sullen looks with broken smiles. I grew curious as to why he was out so late all the time".

Serenity fidgets uncomfortably as Willard continues "imagine my surprise when I found out he was sleeping with one of her best friends. And who was I? Of course, I couldn't tell her at the time. I watched, day after day, lie after lie. This sweet girl being taken advantage of by people she trusted. When William bought the ring, I damn near lost my mind. No, literally, I scoffed so loud in the store I thought they'd kick me out. You know the good thing about surprises? Someone always tells someone. In that moment I decided when and where I would do it. I'd kill him, leave him with a permanent broken smile. And I did. The look of terror on Paisley's face was not one I enjoyed. I watched her looking in my eyes like I was some kind of monster. I wanted to tell her why, but instead, I left. I went about, watching the aftermath of what I'd done. You weren't there for her. Chloe wasn't there for her. Londyn was the only true friend she had. From then on, Paisley changed".

"Well yeah, I would expect so. You stabbed her fiancé to death right in front of her. No telling what you did to her by doing that" Serenity crosses her arms.

"What I did to her was save her from a lifetime of regret by marrying a cheater! You know, I never understood why he proposed. He was clearly getting what he needed elsewhere, why propose?" Willard wears a dumbfounded look.

Serenity lifts her shoulders in a shrug "I don't

know. I guess you could have asked him if you didn't kill him".

"Perhaps" Willard stands from his seated position, placing his empty plate back on the end table.

"So, am I going to sit here and starve all morning or?" Serenity's empty stomach rumbles.

"Ah yes, of course. Where are my manners?" Willard grabs a second plate off the end table, transferring the cold food to a paper plate he can bend between the cell bars.

Serenity carefully sets her plate of food on the wooden floor "So, you seemed pretty upset last night".

"Oh, you heard that?" Willard approaches the window "Yes... well after two years of watching the love of my life, Paisley isn't quite as predictable as I thought she was. I am now at a crossroads. On the one hand, I don't need Jaxon. On the other, Jaxon also saved me the same night Paisley did. I did save him back by killing his brother and".

"Wait you killed his brother!?" Serenity's eyes widen, flabbergasted.

Willard returns to the worn armchair "Yes,

Serenity. I killed his brother. Harvey was a parasite. Sometimes, Jaxon's heart is too big even for him to handle. Jaxon could never be who he was meant to be with Harvey in the way. He should be thanking me, but again, I'm dealing with an ungrateful friend. My problem with Jaxon; I didn't expect he'd be an obstacle to Paisley's heart. I thought it would do me good to have a friend to call on for guy time when Paisley is being a… you know, an annoying bitch like I am certain she can be. But maybe I should have learned from you and William's playbook; don't trust a friend of the opposite sex around your significant other".

Serenity flashes a contempt look as she devours her breakfast.

Willard glances at his phone "Well, as much as I am enjoying this enthralling conversation, it is time for the next phase to begin" he makes a beeline for the door.

"Wait, what's the next phase?" Serenity may as well be talking to herself as Willard is out the door in a flash.

"Whatever… Damnit, he didn't even give me water! Ugh!" she grips her face with her fingertips.

Across the street, after their morning training session, Jaxon and Paisley sit at his dinner table snacking on protein bars.

"You learn quick. I'm impressed with how seamlessly you've picked up the leg sweep" Jaxon places his arms on the table.

Paisley smiles skeptically, resting her chin in her palm "You really think so?".

"Yeah, I do" he wipes his brow "I feel like when my brother taught me all that technical stuff, it took me awhile to grasp it. Maybe I was too impatient or something. But you did good. Sorry it's so hot in here by the way. They still haven't fixed my air conditioner".

"It isn't Kent Gardens if something isn't broken right?" Paisley giggles.

Jaxon scoffs "Ain't that the truth".

Paisley's heart drops when Jaxon's phone rings.

She's relieved when he picks up the video call to a sweet little voice "Uncle Jaxon!" Freya hollers, her face fills the screen.

"Hi sweetie! What are you and mommy doing?" Jaxon takes a sip of water, moving to the end of the table so Paisley can see too.

"We're swimming. I jumped in the big area!" Freya beams.

"Wow, good job! I am so proud of you" Jaxon wears an impressed expression.

"I had a scary dream too" Freya climbs on a pool chair, cuddling up on her mother's lap.

"Aw, you did?" Jaxon makes a sad face, leaning an elbow on the table.

"Yeah, she wanted to call you because she said you're brave and you could make her feel brave too" Morgan chimes in behind her daughter "I told her mommy was braver but she still wanted to call you" Morgan grins mischievously.

Jaxon wears joking glare at his sister "Well I'm glad you called Freya. You are a tough little girl you know that? You're even braver than me when I was little".

Paisley's heart fills with happiness as she watches Jaxon talk to his niece.

"Really!?" Freya's face lights up.

Jaxon threads a hand through his hair "Yes, you are. Let's see how big your muscles are".

Freya gives the phone to her mom and puts her arms up mimicking a flex.

"Wow, those are really big muscles! Yep, you're stronger than any scary dreams. Always remember that sweet baby" Jaxon reassures.

Freya plasters a comforted, cheesy smile on her face "Is that your girlfriend uncle?".

Jaxon feels his face turn scarlet "I don't know, do you think she would like me. I'm kinda weird" Jaxon makes a silly face through the phone.

Freya cracks up laughing "She will like you. You can't be shy uncle. She looks like a princess and princesses are nice, you know that. Do you know what's her name?".

Jaxon chuckles "You're right. Her name is Paisley".

"Ok" Freya giggles.

"Alright, well we'll talk to you later ok?" Jaxon smiles.

"Ok, bye uncle" Freya waves at Jaxon through the phone.

"Bye baby" Jaxon waves back "Love you".

"Love you" Freya responds, hitting the end call button quickly after.

"That was the sweetest thing ever!" Paisley's eyes fill with admiration "she sure adores her uncle".

Jaxon smiles.

"Oh, crap we lost track of time! Londyn just texted me, she's on her way up" Paisley face palms.

She slams her mid-section against the corner of the dining table as she gets up "ouch!" she grabs at her stomach, wincing and laughing.

"Are you ok?" Jaxon tries to hold in a laugh.

Paisley reels in her giggles "I'm ok. I'm used to it. All these scars and bruises on my legs are proof I am far from graceful".

They hurry out the door and up to her apartment.


"Hey girl!" Paisley calls out, her ponytail bouncing.

Londyn gives each of them a once over, pointing her finger between them as she narrows her eyes "You're sweating, he's sweating. And your hair looks like sex hair" Londyn's eyes brighten "Were you guys having sex!?"

"Londyn!" Paisley blushes, smiling as she turns away "No, we did not. We've been training all morning, working on takedowns" Paisley opens her door and the three step inside.

"Oh, I bet you have" Londyn jests with a gentle elbow into Paisley's side.

Paisley chuckles, rolling her eyes "Anyways so, this is Jaxon. Jaxon this is my very forward best friend, Londyn".

"It's nice to meet you Londyn" Jaxon extends his hand.

"It's nice to meet you too" Londyn grabs hold of Jaxon's hand.

Minutes later, Elijah and Bishop arrive.

"Damn, it smells like buttercream and happiness in here!" Elijah breathes in deeply.

His comment draws chuckles from the group and each member is introduced to one another.

Elijah, Bishop, and Jaxon stand next to Paisley's kitchen, conversing "Rough morning?" Elijah cracks a grin.

Jaxon jokingly pushes Elijah, shaking his head, reciprocating a smirk.

"Not to mention you're sober and happy, like uncharacteristically happy" Elijah chuckles "Did she climb over that anger wall of yours?".

"Damn, that's record timing" Bishop adds.

"You guys are such haters" Jaxon tilts his head back, rolling his eyes "She's something though. Who knew the girl Elijah didn't believe existed the other day, would have me captivated the way she does" he gazes at Paisley's dimpled smile, watching her tuck a curl behind her ear as she talks with Londyn on the love seat.

Londyn leans in and whispers to Paisley "Tell me the truth" she glances up at Jaxon "you guys really didn't have sex?".

"We didn't. But we kissed, last night after my show and… on the rooftop" Paisley wears a lopsided grin.

"I knew something was up! Details girl! I need them!" Londyn's whispers grow excited.

Paisley makes a quick glance at the guys walking over "I'll tell you later" she says with a twinkle in her eyes.

"Ugh, horrible timing guys" Londyn pouts "At least tell me... was it good?" Londyn asks, hoping for a teaser.

"Better than good" Paisley flutters her eyelashes dramatically, touching her chin to her shoulder.

Londyn's full lips curve into a smile "Thank you Jaxon" she thinks, overwhelmed with happiness for her best friend.

"So, I guess we'll just dive right in. First things first, what do we even know about this guy?" Bishop scratches his shoulder, pacing in front of the seated group like a teacher "He doesn't come up in any of my databases. The picture you sent me for facial recognition got no hits, nothing. All I got is this punk ass shiner he gave me yesterday".

"Yeah he tried to get me with that too" Jaxon shakes his head, resting his arm on the upholstered armrest.

"I see he must have missed" Bishop scoffs.

"Yep, I didn't miss him though" Jaxon smirks "I beat his ass down, but... I'll admit, he fooled me. Somehow, he knew about Caroline and he used that against me. He told me Paisley was gonna overdose if I didn't make it to her in time".

"Damn, that's cold" Elijah takes off his glasses, cleaning the lenses on his shirt.

"I still can't believe I was almost murdered yesterday" Londyn's eyes dart between Jaxon and Bishop "I knew something about the way he looked at me felt conniving, but I never would have guessed he had blood on his mind".

"Wait so, am I the only one out of the loop here? What's this guy look like?" Elijah's eyes like a deer in headlights.

Jaxon pulls up the photos he took of the glossy pictures Willard had in his cardboard box "My bad bro, I thought I sent it to you".

Elijah accepts the phone from Jaxon, looking at the picture of Willard, he cracks up with laughter "Damn, he's looking desperate AND creepy. Who takes a picture of themselves pretending to kiss someone in the background?".

"So weird" Paisley shudders.

Elijah passes the phone to Bishop's outstretched hand.

Bishop begins looking through the photos, placing a finger to his chin "I'm not going to find anything I don't want to see in here am I, Jaxon?" he chuckles.

"There might be a couple shirtless selfies in there if you go too far, nothing you ain't seen before though" Jaxon laughs, leaning back against the cushioned sofa.

"Ha ha you got jokes" Bishop stops swiping for a second before his thumb continues moving between pictures, a thinking stare on his face "These pictures of Paisley in her apartment, they're all taken at the same angle" he gets up and approaches her window "If I was a betting man, I'd bet he has a spot in that vacant building over there".

"Damn" Jaxon joins Bishop "I hadn't even

thought about that".

"So, he could have been across the street this whole time?" Paisley's expression concerns.

"As much as I hate to say it, it's possible. If he is, he would have a view right into your apartment. Do you know how long that building has been vacant?" Bishop turns his back to the window.

Paisley presses her finger to her bottom lip "Umm, maybe a year, year and a half or so? They used to be these crappy apartments. I overheard a conversation the manager of Kent Gardens had; he said someone bought the building out with supposed intentions of restoring them, but nothing's been done since the buyout".

Paisley's phone rings "Oh my gosh, every time I get a call now, I'm so jumpy. I feel like it's Willard calling. Thankfully, it's just work. I have to take this really quick".

"You're good, I'm going to step out and make a quick call as well" Bishop starts towards Paisley's front door.

Paisley walks to the kitchen "Gina, hey what's up?".

"Hey Paisley, sorry to bother you, but have you heard from Macie today? She didn't show up for her shift this morning and hasn't answered any of my calls or texts".

Paisley's heart rate quickens "No, I haven't heard from her. I'll try to give her a call. Please let me know if you get a hold of her Gina".

"Ok thanks Paisley, I will" Gina hangs up.

Paisley quickly tries calling Macie "Come on, pick it up Macie" she thinks but there's no answer.

She tries again, still no answer.

Paisley slowly approaches the group, spaced out to a nightmare scenario.

"Is everything ok, Paisley?" Londyn looks up at Paisley standing behind the sofa.

"He's got Macie. I'm sure of it" Paisley closes her eyes and leans her palms on the back of the sofa.

"What do you mean?" Londyn questions as Bishop reenters the apartment, tucking his phone into his pocket.

"That was Gina. Macie didn't show up for work this morning and isn't answering her phone. If he really does have her, he's going to kill her, just like he did Chloe".

Jaxon rounds the arm of the couch, taking her in his arms "Hey, he's not going to kill anyone. We're going to put a plan together. We're taking him down today".

"He wants to break us, right?" Paisley's eyes watch Jaxon's.

Jaxon nods as Paisley draws a nervous breath "What if we let him. Me in particular? He's obviously infatuated with me. If I'm over there, that could distract him enough for you guys to get in and search the floor you think he's on without tipping him off and then bust in and arrest him" she turns her attention to Bishop "how sure are you with picking out what floor he's on?".

"Ninety percent?" Bishop rubs the back of his head.

"You're not seriously considering baiting yourself are you!?" Londyn stands, crossing her arms over her chest "I mean when I told you, you were fierce, I didn't mean for you to throw yourself into a room alone with a lunatic" Londyn hard sighs.

"I know. I'm terrified just thinking about it. But I

have to do this. I need to... for Macie. For you guys... for me. Londyn, Willard was so close to taking you away. And now, if I don't do something, he may succeed with Macie. There's no telling who he will go for next. I'm beginning to realize, if we're going to stop him, I can't sit on the bench. I'm the best option to throw him off. My anxiety, my fear, it's controlling me, killing me. I just want him gone. Maybe then, I could be me again. I've got an idea... Just hear me out. In his eyes, I'm this vulnerable girl who doesn't have the heart to fight back, I'm easy to manipulate, I'm the perfect victim. With me, I'm certain he would let his guard and he would never see me coming. I'm like... a secret weapon" she scoffs gently, trying to make light of the situation.

Londyn breathes deep and slow, her hardened expression softens "I don't like the idea at all. But that doesn't mean I'm not proud of you girl. I'm stunned, I suppose in a good way. Witnessing your bravery surface again, it's heartwarming. Frustrating too because obviously I don't want you in danger, but I get it" Londyn wears a gentle smile, approaching and hugging Paisley.

"Thank you for understanding. Now, I just have to convince him I'm broken. My acting skills suck so, there's that" Paisley's comment draws light laughter "I don't even know what I would do when I'm in his presence".

"The biggest thing is, don't get too comfortable. Keep your guard up. He may claim to care about you, and I don't want to scare you, but we don't know what he will do when he's got you alone" Bishop sets his mouth in a hard line.

Paisley swallows uncomfortably.

"Hey, if it comes down to it" Jaxon grabs hold of her wrists, holding her hands up like a fighter preparing for a fight "these are your lifelines. You have a fire burning inside, use that fire, don't let it use you. No doubt, he'll try to get in your head. You've got to do your best not to let him. I know we haven't got to train as much as we'd like to before you're thrown in a position like this, but you've got power in your hands, and your leg sweep is impressive. He bleeds just like you do. Make him bleed".

Paisley nods, her doe-eyes watch Jaxon's hazel iris's as he continues "Just remember, we have an idea where he is, we'll be coming for you shortly after he takes you".

"Is there anything about Chloe's murder that might help us be prepared for what he might put you through though?" Elijah crosses his ankles in front of him, his forearms resting on the arms of the easy chair.

The butterflies in Paisley's stomach grow wild as a video call comes through on her phone.

"Being brave was so much easier before it became real" she thinks, certain this time it is Willard calling.

Comfort surrounds her as the group closes in.

A slow breath in, a slow breath out, she swipes to answer, afraid Macie may already be dead.

"Hello beautiful" Willard's smile makes her sick "Hey, we've got the whole crew today haven't we. Good, because I've got quite a show. For those of you who missed last night's show, you're in luck. Today's will be better. And we shouldn't have any outbursts from Serenity this time. Her mouth is stapled shut".

"Oh my gosh!" Paisley gasps.

"Sorry, but she had no right speaking to you the way she did last night. Now, back to business. Macie sure put up quite a fight, but she didn't have it in her to win" Willard faces the camera at Macie, drugged and handcuffed against the same wall Chloe was murdered against "so".

"Please don't hurt her Willard!" Paisley interrupts, her voice a desperate plea "She's done nothing wrong other than knowing me. I get it now, why you're doing what you're doing. I may not be as broken as you want me, but I am still broken regardless. Please, just take me in place of her. I can't bear the thought of someone else dying because of me".

"But Paisley, that means you still care. I don't want you to care. I told you, I would break you. Then and only then, will I accept your friendship because, to put it simply, I don't trust you. How could I trust someone who's sleeping with my best friend?" Willard's expression dulls.

"What are you talking about?" Paisley glances silently at her friends.

"Last night, I watched you and Jaxon together. I saw you wrap your arms around him. Next thing I know, the lights are out" Willard huffs.

"We didn't sleep together Willard. Not that it would be any of your business if we did. Look, I know I'm not as broken as you hoped I would be. But you've watched me, you know me. What do you lose by trading Macie for me? You can still break me if I'm your captive. I just… I don't want any more innocent people to die. It's not right, you know that. Even YOU can't be that heartless, right Willard?" Paisley sweetens her husky voice.

Willard watches her innocent stare; he's got no defense for her sweetened voice as the goosebumps take over his arms "Perhaps you're right. Perhaps not... Give me a moment to ponder, and I'll call you back".

Willard hangs up abruptly.

"Do you think he bought it?" Paisley asks nervously.

"Girl, I almost bought it. I'm pretty sure he did" Londyn wears a reassuring smile.

Paisley sighs with relief.

"Was Chloe handcuffed and drugged as well?" Bishop narrows his pondering, detective eyes.

"She definitely had her hands cuffed in front her. She seemed disoriented but I'm not sure if it was from the gash he carved into her face before he called or if he drugged her. What are you thinking?" Jaxon asks.

Bishop rubs his chin "If he's a creature of habit, and likely he is, he'll drug and cuff Paisley as well".

Paisley's eyes dart nervously between Londyn and Jaxon as Bishop continues "What are the chances you've ever tried to pick the lock on a pair of handcuffs?".

"No chance at all" she shakes her head.

"That's alright, you've bought us a little time before he calls back. A few practice runs and you'll get it. It's easier than it sounds. Do you have those little things that you girls stick in your hair that holds it in place or something? Damn, what is it called" Bishop looks to Londyn and Paisley for help.

"A bobby pin?" Londyn giggles.

"Yes! That's it. Ok so grab a few of those and I'll show you how to do it" Bishop says proudly.

"My vanity is littered with stray bobby pins" Paisley begins to walk towards her room.

"I got some right here girl, don't worry" Londyn pulls a few out of her hair and hands them to Bishop.

"Ok so first, we've got to get rid of this end piece" Bishop begins to show her as Jaxon and Elijah strike up a conversation.

"Are you sure letting her go in is going to be the

best option? I know we're pressed for time, but" Elijah gives an unsure shrug.

Jaxon strokes his stubbled chin "Do you remember when I got out of the hospital after the shooting and you told me I needed to face Bishop and talk to him about what I thought I saw?".

Elijah nods, Jaxon continues "I should have listened to you. I wasted years of friendship because I was stubborn and angry. It was like I had grown accustomed to messed up shit happening that I didn't see any other way. What I'm getting at though is, she needs to face Willard. Yeah, he killed Harvey, he fucked with my life too. It felt good sending my knuckles to his face. She needs that as well. She needs to take control and take her life back. This is her way of doing that, whether she realizes it or not. And I don't wanna take that from her, you know?".

"I get that. Damn, look at you bro. Getting all soft and stuff" Elijah pokes fun.

Jaxon smirks and playfully punches Elijah "Man, whatever".

"Hey bro" Elijah's voice grows sincere "I know we joke and stuff, but you do seem a lot better. It's nice to see that".

"I am bro, I am" Jaxon claps Elijah's shoulder.

"Hey guys" Paisley holds up her phone "he's calling back".

Paisley answers Willard's video call and waits nervously for his answer.

Willard breathes a hard breath "Alright, I've racked my brain over and again. You'll be happy to know I've made my decision. Though, I'd like to talk to Jaxon first".

Paisley wears a puzzled expression as she hands the phone to Jaxon.

"Jaxon, my friend, or shall I say, my former friend. I wanted to see the look on your face when I tell you I'm agreeing to take Paisley away. I know you'd like her for yourself, but she just isn't the right one for you. She belongs with me Jaxon. She always has. Killing William was a favor to her but you… well, you were a mere unexpected obstacle" Willard guides a drugged Macie down a littered stairwell "I suppose you can see; I always get what I want… eventually of course".

Jaxon glares through the phone "Nah, let's call it what it is Willard. You are selfish and your logic is twisted. Yeah maybe she WAS being cheated on. But you took away her right to make her own decision. Certainly, it would have been less traumatic than watching someone die. Certainly, she would have recovered from the heartbreak. It blows my mind that you actually believe you did her a favor".

"How am I selfish Jaxon?" a line appears between Willard's brows.

"How are you selfish? Really? Instead of bettering yourself to fit in her world, you'd rather break her to fit in yours. That's not the mark of someone who cares. If you care like you say you do, you'd stop what you're doing, turn yourself in, and just face the consequences".

"Well, you know what Jaxon, you've enlightened me. I think I'll do just that. I've seen the error in my ways, and you know, I... I just feel so bad" Willard chuckles facetiously "let's give the phone back to Paisley already, so I can get this over with Jaxon".

Jaxon covers his eyes with a hand, giving the phone back to Paisley "I can't wait to see the look on your face when your game is over" he thinks.

"Yes Willard? I'm here, you said you decided. The suspense is killing me so can we just get on with it" Paisley can't hide the agitation in her voice.

"Of course. Now, let me tell you how this works. There's absolutely no room for negotiation. It is my way, or I continue with my original plan and my knife disappears into Macie's flesh. Is that understood?" Willard focuses his empty eyes through the screen into Paisley's.

She makes a quick glance around the room "Ok, Willard, understood. May I make one request though, as a friend?".

Willard raises a bushy brow, giving her the go ahead.

"Please don't drug me. I would hate to start off our friendship under the idea that we couldn't trust each other" Paisley chews at a fingernail.

Willard takes a pondering second before closing his eyes and pinching the bridge of his nose "Ok, I suppose I can see where you're coming from. Of course, you'll understand I need you handcuffed at the very least".

"Yes, that makes sense" Paisley feels slightly relieved.

"There's an alley behind Kent Gardens, I'm certain you're familiar?" Willard paces the area.

Paisley nods as he continues "You'll come alone. Macie will be free to go as soon as I have you restrained and in the back of the car. You'll send a text to Londyn to let her know the exchange has been made and then your phone will be no longer. No worries, I'll provide you with a replacement just as soon as you've proven yourself to me. If there's any attempt to foil what I've laid out, Macie dies. If I see the police, Macie dies. If I hear police sirens, Macie dies. If I... well you get it, right?".

"No one is going to try anything" Paisley assures.

"I should hope not. More like, Macie will hope not. Ten minutes, Paisley" Willard hangs up.

"I'm so nervous. What if it doesn't work? I don't know why I felt so confident before, now I'm just jittery" Paisley bounces on her toes.

"You're good, it's just your adrenaline" Jaxon holds her hand in his "You've got this, be confident. He's a coward, you're brave".

Paisley nods, facing the group like an unsure substitute teacher "If I don't come back".

"Girl don't talk like that! You're going to make me cry and you know I don't cry" Londyn squints her eyes, hoping her tears don't ignore the effort to stop them.

"I'm sorry, but I have to. At the very least it will make me feel better" Paisley takes a deep breath, facing Londyn "If I don't come back, promise me you'll find another best friend to make inappropriate jokes with and who appreciates you for the incredible friend you are" Paisley turns her attention to Jaxon, holding his hand "Promise me, you'll apply for the art school so you can become a rich, famous artist one day" she glances between Elijah and Bishop "and you two, promise me you'll keep them in line".

Paisley's speech draws nods of agreement.

"Now it's my turn" Jaxon gazes into her eyes "when you DO come back, you and I are taking a trip to Georgia".

Paisley smiles lightly "Deal!".

Elijah calls Paisley over and after a brief conversation, she makes her rounds of hugs and waves goodbye, shutting the door to her apartment, and making her way to the graffitied alley behind Kent Gardens.

# Chapter Eleven

"This is too surreal" Paisley thinks, waiting alone in the alley "birds are singing, people hustling from place to place, a bright blue sky. Just another day for millions of people. People who haven't had the misfortune of saving Willard and becoming his obsession. Why did" Paisley's thoughts are interrupted by Willard's hand around her mouth, he pulls her behind a trash bin.

"Scream and Macie dies" he turns Paisley to face him "Now put this on and keep your head down" he hands her a baseball cap as he slaps the handcuffs around her wrists.

"Wait, where's Macie!?" Paisley asks, trying to keep up with her breaths and Willard's pace leading her through the alley.

"You won't be texting Londyn, Jaxon, or anyone for that matter" He takes her phone and tosses it against a brick wall "Macie is in the neighboring alley, cuffed to a scaffolding. I'll be sending Jaxon a text to retrieve her when we get to where we're going".

Paisley focuses her eyes on the sidewalk as they turn into an alley she assumes is connected to the old apartments across the street from Kent Gardens, although if they are, he took an alternate route. Willard leads her to a pair of cellar doors.

Paisley steps onto a creaky, wooden stair and hesitates "Wait where are we go".

Willard pushes her forward "Keep going Paisley, we are nearly there".

"No wait, I" Paisley pushes her back into Willard, trying to stop her momentum but he pushes her again.

Paisley slips down the small staircase, tumbling to the bottom. She winces in pain; the baseball cap flies off during her fall. Willard slams the cellar door shut, leaving only the light from a few lightbulbs that obviously have no business lighting up a room.

Paisley frantically pushes herself backwards, her shoes having a difficult time not slipping on the dirty concrete. She watches Willard walk right past her and over to an area nearby Serenity sitting against a wall behind iron bars.

"Her mouth isn't stapled shut" Paisley thinks, the sound of water dripping from leaky pipes into grimy puddles growing louder by the drip.

Serenity can't hide her frustration "I'm so sick of moving from cell to cell. Just get it over with already. Kill me or don't. I'm hungry, I'm thirsty, I'm tired".

"Shut up!" Willard fires at Serenity, silencing her.

Paisley sits against the cracked concrete wall, wide-eyed and nervous. She notices a pair of shackles attached to the wall.

"Where am I?" She thinks, shivering in the cold

room that smells of mildew and rotted wood.

"Do you know why I killed William, Paisley?" Willard's tone lifeless.

"He was cheating on me?" Paisley's voice trembles.

"Deceit" Willard answers, his back turned as he fiddles with something on the table he stands in front of "I absolutely despise deception".

"Ok, I... umm, I understand that" Paisley stammers.

"No, you don't!" Willard turns around, anger now evident on his face "You deceived me. Well, at least you thought you did. The fact is you tried to. It's written all over your face. You expected to be somewhere else because they were supposed to save the poor damsel in distress. I suppose I could place some blame on myself as well. Somewhere along the way, I showed my hand. Your friends would never have allowed you to sacrifice yourself for Macie if they didn't know where they could find you".

Paisley's heartbeat pounds as Willard continues "Well, I warned Jaxon not to underestimate me. But he did, didn't he?" Willard waits for an answer, but a blank stare is all he gets "DIDN'T

HE!?" Willard yells.

"Y..yes " Paisley's handcuffs shake lightly.

Willard struts towards Paisley, a steak knife in his hand "Yes. I wonder what will be going through his anger management deprived mind when he finds out the room he's so sure you're in… is empty" Willard chuckles, a conniving grin surfaces.

Paisley swallows uncomfortably, eyeing the knife in Willard's grasp.

Willard catches her glance between him and the knife "Oh this?" he presents the knife, bending to Paisley's level and grabbing her hair.

Her breaths quicken, she tries leaning back away from the knife.

"Yes, I should stick this so far in your stomach it gets lost" Willard grits his teeth, loosening his grip on her hair and rising back to his feet "Oh but I won't. No, this is for the steak I've prepared for us. No doubt you'll want your steak cut into pieces".

Paisley hangs her head "I'm sorry I tried to trick you" she watches Serenity peering at her as she moves her cuffed hands to her hair, digging the bobby pin out while Willard's back is turned.

Willard stops cutting into Paisley's steak and turns to look at her. She tries to remain inconspicuous, burying her hands in her lap, hoping he didn't notice her subtle startled jump.

Willard sighs and returns to cutting her steak "You were scared, I understand that. Of course, I can let it slide this once. I apologize for pushing you down the stairs. I let my frustration get the better of me. I just don't like to use this room unless absolutely necessary. We could have had much nicer accommodations, something more fit for the stubborn love of my life. But for now, we get the cellar. No worries though, with you by my side, no matter where I am, I can only count myself lucky".

Serenity rolls her eyes. Paisley works the lock, finding it harder and harder to breathe as she tries to control her anxiety.

Willard turns, startling her again.

"Shit" she mumbles.

He grabs the plates and starts her way. She drops the bobby pin between her crossed legs and gives a half smile as he hands her the plate of food.

He sits on the floor across her, setting his plate in front of him.

"Umm what am I? Chopped liver?" Serenity throws her hands up in disgust.

Willard stares Serenity down "Let's not forget why you are in this position dear Serenity. You are not here because I like you. You are here to die".

"How can he say that so nonchalantly, like her life doesn't even matter" Paisley thinks, glaring at him while he's still focused on Serenity.

"How can you be so unbothered by killing people Willard? I mean, you say you care about me and even cared for Jaxon so, there must be a small part of you that has some humanity?" Paisley treads carefully.

Willard rubs his forehead, running his palm down his face "My humanity? After you saved me, I watched, night after night as William disappointed you. The late night calls where I could only assume, by the look on your face, he was going to be "out late" Willard gestures quotation marks "He was with HER" Willard points at Serenity, giving her a dirty look "For every night he left you alone, I was there. I saw your tears. I heard you cry".

"Heard?" Paisley interrupts, tilting her head to the side.

"Oh yes" Willard scoffs "Paisley, you didn't lock your doors, your windows, your car. How naïve you were to danger back then. A complete one-eighty from today's version of Paisley. There were many times you knew someone was inside, but you kept yourself in denial. You blew it off, told yourself you were hearing things. Which I suppose was true, you just didn't realize you were hearing me. Oh, many times, if you had only turned the corner or opened the closet door, I would have had some SPLAINING TO DO" Willard does his best Ricky Ricardo impression, cracking himself up as he takes a bite of bleeding steak.

"Splainin'" Serenity interrupts from her cell.

"Excuse me?" Willard's face goes blank, he turns his head towards Serenity.

"Splainin' is how he says it, not splaining. You put too much emphasis on the g at the end. If you're going to do it, do it right" Serenity crosses her arms, leaning against the disheveled wall.

Willard stops chewing, sets his fork down, and grabs a napkin. He removes the piece of half-chewed steak from his mouth into his napkin and rises to a standing position.

"You know what Serenity? If you want to be

involved in the conversation so badly, let's hear it. I, and certainly Paisley is as well, am dying to know how you and William ended up entangled in dirty linen" Willard glances at Paisley.

Paisley looks away "I'd be lying if I didn't say I was at least curious" she thinks, moving her contempt stare from the dirty ground to Serenity.

Serenity moves to the corner of her cell and slides her back down the wall to a seated position, crushing a beetle that didn't scurry away quick enough "What is there to explain? It happened, he's dead, she's alive, I'll probably be dead soon. Who cares why?".

"There's a grilled chicken breast and baked macaroni and cheese from Michelangelo's with your name on it for the story" Willard presses his hands in a steeple, bringing his index fingers to his lips.

Serenity's empty stomach grumbles at the thought of food, she exhales a sigh "Throw a bottle of water in and you've got a deal".

"There's the spirit!" Willard stands to retrieve the food and water for Serenity.

She takes a quick bite and a long gulp of water "To put it simply, Paisley, he was bored. Of course, he cared about you, but he felt trapped. You were too sweet and innocent. He couldn't break your heart and leave you so, he stayed, got what he needed elsewhere, and settled with you. I don't know why the fuck he proposed to you".

Paisley feels her heart tug "Keep it together" she thinks before speaking "I don't get it. You were the one friend of mine he never liked. He always said you were too crazy, and he didn't trust you".

Serenity brings her water to her lips, giving Paisley a puppy dog pout "Oh is that what he told you? That's not what he told me while we were".

"Alright we get it" Willard interrupts.

Serenity throws a devious smile at Paisley before taking another bite of chicken.

"Every time he would say something like that, I defended you. How stupid I must have looked" Paisley shakes her head, sadness clouds her features "How long?".

"How long what?" Serenity looks up from her plate.

"How long were you sleeping with him!? Don't

play dumb!" Paisley shouts.

Serenity raises her shoulder in a half shrug "A few weeks or so? I didn't make a pass at him until my mother died. If only you guys hadn't walked in when you did, things might have been different. It's possible she would still be alive. William may not have strayed, well at least not with me. I don't know, maybe I shouldn't have blamed you for my mother's death, but I did. I wanted to hurt you and stealing him away from you was the only way I knew how".

"But you hated your mom!" Paisley's eyes burn with frustration "and so what if we came inside that day, what would that have changed Serenity!? Why do you think she would still be alive!? Did you kill her?" Paisley feels dirty even asking the question.

Serenity hops up and approaches the edge of the cell "What did you just say?".

Paisley's heart rate rises "Did you kill your mother, Serenity?".

"Are you trying to find out if you could stomach killing me? Maybe if you knew I was a bad person, you could convince yourself to do it?" Serenity's face contorts with disgust "Of course I didn't kill her. She did it to herself".

"What does that mean?" Paisley's emerald eyes narrow.

Perturbed, Serenity sighs "She was getting better. She was supposed to be sober and we were supposed to try mending things. Not that she deserved it, but she was my mother and she was all I had besides you guys so, I wanted it to work out. Stupid me, I know. But when I got there, she wasn't just off the wagon, she destroyed the damn thing. And then not too long after, you guys walked in. I was just trying to scare her like she scared me all those years. That's all. But when I watched you guys leave; I was distracted long enough that she lunged up at me. Her hands had never gripped my throat so hard. I swung the bottle at her head and knocked her out. At least that's what I thought. I left her there, lying on the floor. I figured she would come to later. But when I went back to check on her after the bar, she was still lying there. That's when I knew I killed her. So, like I said, if you guys hadn't walked in, she probably wouldn't have attacked me, and I definitely wouldn't have busted her head open with a liquor bottle".

"Excuse us for not being able to see through walls and read your mind" Paisley looks down at her food.

"Do you need a Kleenex?" Willard cuts in sarcastically "That was… touching".

Serenity rolls her eyes and sits back down in front of her plate.

Willard tilts his head and leans towards a spaced-out Paisley "Penny for your thoughts?"

Paisley snaps out of it "Nothing Willard".

"Are you still holding out hope your Jaxon is going to come bursting through those cellar doors to save his precious princess?" Willard shakes his head in annoyance "Let me make something clear because damnit if you didn't write the book on overthinking! You don't walk out of here until Serenity is lying in a pool of blood created by you. And when you do walk out, it'll be hand in hand with me. Now if you'll excuse me, I've got a 1967 Cabernet with our names on it".

"It's now or never" she thinks, watching Willard walk away.

She sneaks a glance at Serenity "Ok good, she's not paying attention, no doubt she would rat me out now".

Paisley rushes the bobby pin back between her fingers, taking quick looks between Willard and the cuffs as she maneuvers her key to freedom.

"Come on" she thinks "Ugh this was so much easier when Bishop was watching me do it".

Her heart nearly jumps out of her chest as a single strand of the handcuff slides out, exposing a scratched up but freed wrist "Oh my gosh!", she hurries to remove the next one, her hands shaking.

Paisley's eyes well up with happy tears as the next cuff comes undone.

She moves her plate to her palms, hiding her unrestrained wrists as she rises to her feet "Willard, where do you want me to put my food at? I'm finished".

"Oh, here let me get that for you dear" Willard carefully approaches with two wine-filled glasses, setting one down on a cluttered shelf, ready to accept Paisley's plate.

"You've barely touched your food" Willard's voice concerns "Are you sure you've had enough?".

"Oh, I've had quite enough of you" she leaves the words in her head, giving only a subtle nod.

Willard goes to grab her plate. She goes for the element of surprise, letting it go and rearing her closed fist back, swinging for the fences.

The plate shatters at Willard's feet, Paisley's knuckles breeze by his face as he dodges back and shoves her.

Her elbows scrape the ground, she grimaces.

"You sneaky bitch!" Willard sets his glass of wine next to the other one, unbuttoning his top button, rolling his neck in a circle "You do not want to do this Paisley and I do not want to hurt you. Calm down, let's get you back in the handcuffs, and we'll forget your outburst".

Adrenaline pulses through Paisley's veins, she pushes herself to her feet and rushes Willard. He steps aside and throws her to the ground again.

"Ah" she can't hide the pain as she slams against the wall.

"After everything I've done for you and this is how you repay me?" Willard places his hands on his hips, beside himself.

"Everything you've done for me?" Paisley scoffs, standing to her feet, holding a hand over her bruised ribs "You haven't done anything for me! Everything you did, you did for yourself and your own selfish reasons! I used to smile; you took that away from me. I used to feel safe and secure; you took that away too. I'm done letting you run around in my head. Living in fear... in paranoia... anxiety attacks always lurking beneath the surface. I'm sick of it".

"So, you're going to stand up and face your fears now, is that it? You get a little taste of bravery and suddenly you're a fearless woman?" Willard guffaws "No Paisley, that's not how this works. No, you'll always be the girl who pulls into a parking spot and leaves seconds later because something doesn't feel right. You'll always be the girl who steps into a building and immediately looks for all the exits because it's inevitable that you'll be kidnapped or murdered by some random stranger. Just accept it. Without me, little dove, you will always be an anxious, paranoid mess".

"Maybe you're right, Willard" Paisley walks towards him, her fists in a tight ball "One thing I won't be though, is YOURS" Paisley swings for his jaw.

Willard side-steps again and hooks his knuckles into her cheekbone. Paisley falls to her hands and knees. Her hair falls over her shoulders, covering her face and the blood dripping from Willard's strike.

"Look what you made me do! I told you I did not want to hurt you! Why do you insist on pissing me off?" he bends to her level, sweetening his voice "Come on, let me help you up" he wraps her arm around his neck as he lifts her "I hope you can see that beating me is not an option. Whether you like it or not, this is where you belong. Now, let's get you some ice" he leads her towards a cooler.

"Use that fire, don't let the fire use you" Jaxon's advice replays in Paisley's lowered head.

She grins, takes in a deep breath, and wraps her hands around Willard's arms so tight her nails dig into his skin. She quickly faces him, pulls him towards her, and sweeps his leg, sending them crashing to the ground. Willard slams his head against the concrete, throwing him into a daze.

Paisley mounts and sends a clobbering blow to his jaw.

Tears trickle down her cheeks as she grabs hold of his shirt and continues to bloody her knuckles against his face, every strike like a piece of her being put back together "My life collapsed around me because of you!" she throws a jab to his nose "But MY life is no longer YOURS to toy with!" her bruised and bloodied knuckles continue turning Willard's face purple and red.

"Either kill him or cuff him and let's get out of here Paisley!" Serenity yells from the cell.

Paisley looks up, her brows snap together as she glares at Serenity.

Serenity throws her hands in the air "Look, I'm sorry ok. Let's work it out later? When we're not in some psycho's cellar" Serenity's voice urgent.

Paisley winces through one more crushing blow to Willard's battered face, letting go of his shirt and letting his head fall to the ground. She stands, kicking his weak, outstretched hand. She hurries to the handcuffs just steps away and tightens one end around Willard's wrist, the other end to a link on the nearby shackles.

"Where's the keys at?" she hollers at Serenity, searching a lone table full of junk.

"I don't know. It's got to be up there somewhere" Serenity paces her cell.

Paisley frantically searches, knocking things to the floor "Found them! At least, I hope. There's a few different keys on this key ring".

Willard lets out a wheezing cough, spitting blood as Paisley begins testing the keys "I will never forget you Paisley".

She pauses, vague memories pour into her head so quick it was like she was compelled to forget until those words came out "You said that... the night I saved you".

"You do remember!?" Willard's eyes light up.

"No. I don't remember you, Willard. What I remember is standing up for a timid, weak little man and I remember the feeling I had after those words left your mouth" Paisley stares through Willard.

"The feeling of true love and admiration for the brave woman who stopped three monsters?" Willard looks desperately at Paisley.

"No, Willard. The sick, slimy feeling in the pit of my stomach. The one that told me YOU were the monster" she breaks her gaze from his eyes and goes back to finding the key to unlock Serenity's cell.

Willard sits up "I may rot in prison for the rest of my life, but I will think about you every day. I can only hope you will never forget me".

Paisley twists the next key and hears the lock click before she looks back at Willard's pathetic face "Of course I will. You're forgettable... remember?".

"Finally!" Serenity applauds as Paisley pulls the cell door open "I'm so happy I could kiss you!".

"Please don't" Paisley leans away from Serenity's hug.

"I've only ever wanted people to be happy. Not one person I killed died in sadness. Each was given a permanent grin. It's too bad I'll never get to give you yours, Paisley" Willard's weak voice mutters.

"Yeah, well maybe Jaxon can" Paisley says matter of factly.

Paisley hurries across the room and up the creaky, wooden stairs. She slides the bolted lock out of its locked position and throws the cellar doors open. Fresh air and bright sun welcome her back to freedom. She sighs with relief, taking in a chaotic scene of flashing lights and police searching the area.

Dirty and wet, scraped and bruised, and overwhelmed with emotion, she collapses in the alley, crying, then laughing, then crying "It's over" she says aloud "It's finally over".

Serenity looks up the stairs, sunlight now shining into the dusty room through the open cellar doors. She turns and flashes a devious smile at Willard, walking to the junk table where a roll of duct tape sits next to the knife he used to kill Chloe. She slices a piece of duct tape off, grips the knife, and approaches a worn-down Willard.

She steps on his free hand and bites her bottom lip "Oh, poor Willy" she slaps the duct tape across his mouth "look how helpless you are" she runs the blade across his neck "Are you still curious what I whisper to Paisley before I wake from my nightmares?".

Willard pants nervously as she continues "I promise her..." Serenity leans in, pressing her lips gently against his ear "she's going to die... slowly... painfully" Serenity giggles, moving back away from his ear, boring her eyes into his "They make custom straight-jackets for girls like me. You would have seen it, if you weren't so focused on Paisley. But noooo, everyone is ALWAYS focused on HER. It's ironic isn't it? You meant to break her but instead you brought out a part of me that, I guess, had been hiding for a while. You should have killed me while you had the chance. Oh well" she shrugs "You're not going to rot in prison though silly... you're going to rot right here".

Serenity grins mischievously and shoves Willard's knife into his neck over and again. Blood covers the knife, splattering the floor and her face. Serenity rises to her feet, begins to walk away, and turns to blow Willard a kiss while he struggles through the last seconds of his life.

# Chapter Twelve

Paisley rests her elbows back on the stairs of the concrete stoop, wincing slightly from her fresh scrapes "You guys, seriously, thank you for believing in me".

Londyn gleams, leaning her forearm on an iron railing "I can't get over the fact that I have a badass best friend who just stood up to her stalker and single handedly beat his ass".

"I swear his face looks worse than mine" Paisley's laugh wrinkles her nose.

"Oh, I bet it does" Jaxon inspects Paisley's knuckles.

Elijah crosses his arms over his chest "Man, when we found out Willard owned this building, and Jaxon and I were standing there staring at a blood-stained wall and an empty cell, it was hard not to think the worst".

"That's for sure. We're all proud of you. You were brave and you saved yourself, like we knew you could" Jaxon leans on the iron railing, opposite Londyn.

"Yeah, I mean at one point, I thought for sure he was going to kill me. I don't know how he put it together that we knew where he was, but he was pissed. Threw me down the stairs and held a knife inches from my neck. To say I was terrified is an understatement. After that, I wasn't even sure if what Elijah and I planned was going to work anymore" Paisley's eyes widen.

"Y'all had a plan?" Jaxon wears a curious expression.

"Sure did. This cut right here on my cheekbone is the remnants of a plan that foiled a lovesick asshole" Paisley proudly grins.

"I have to hear this, what was the plan?" Londyn

scratches her neck.

Paisley shoves her blonde curls back away from her face "Elijah told me, if Willard cares about me like he says he does, he won't want to hurt me. And if I can push him enough to throw a punch and hit me, I would have him where I wanted him".

"Yep, you ever seen someone you care about get hit? What's the first thing you do?" Elijah chimes in, looking at each member over the top of his glasses.

"Make sure they're ok" Bishop answers, joining the circle.

"And that's what he did. He helped me up and that's when I knew his guard was down enough. I had one shot at the move we practiced, and I nailed it. Of course, after many failed attempts at just slugging him in his annoying face" Paisley chuckles.

"Well damn, good thinking Elijah" Jaxon claps him on his shoulder.

"You guys want to form a vigilante group and go fight crime now? I've got an alter ego already. She's a billionaire so, we could have some pretty cool outfits... and weapons. Maybe even a secret lair" Paisley jokes, raising her eyebrows.

Londyn rolls her eyes "Who IS this girl?".

Paisley flutters her eyelashes dramatically "Oh hey, did you guys find Macie!?".

"Yeah, we got her. She was a little shaken up but she's ok" Londyn assures.

"Thank goodness" Paisley sighs happily, sitting up.

The group gets quiet when Bishop's partner, Jones, approaches and whispers something in his ear. Jones walks away, the group eyes Bishop waiting for news.

Bishop takes a second "Wow. So, interesting development. Willard is dead, stabbed in the neck multiple times. Serenity and the murder weapon have disappeared".

"I can't say that I don't feel a greater sense of relief hearing that" Paisley rubs a temple with her fingertips.

"Yeah me too" Londyn toys with a lock of hair "But Serenity? Really? She's wild but I wouldn't have dreamed she had THAT in her".

"I don't know, I mean, she spent a lot of time

with Willard. Just the amount of time I was with him was enough for me to want to wring his neck" Paisley gives a half-shrug.

"Well, I don't know about you guys, but I could use some drinks" Londyn moves her eyes along the group of friends.

"Girl I'm a mess, I've got dirt and water and blood" Paisley inspects her arms and hands.

"Take a shower with Jaxon later" Londyn interrupts with a jesting grin.

Paisley rolls her eyes and rises to her feet, fine a couple drinks" she laughs.

Paisley snuggles up to Jaxon, nestles her head onto his shoulder, and takes in the sexy scent of his fiji and palm tree scented body wash after the passionate shower they shared.

"Great idea, Londyn" she thinks with a soft grin.

Jaxon kisses her forehead and wraps her in his arms "Tomorrow, let's start planning our trip to Georgia".

Paisley tilts her head up, swimming in Jaxon's

hazel eyes "I would love that" she locks her lips to his.

Jaxon and Paisley lay tangled in his bedsheets, comforted in each other's embrace, smitten that for the first time in a long time, the future looks bright.

Serenity stands under a moonlit graveyard, staring at a pair of headstones "Well your daughter did it. She stood up to her tormentor and I will admit it was impressive" Serenity takes a cross-legged seat on the cold grass "It really IS a shame you're not here anymore. The fire wasn't meant for you, it was meant for her. You two were the parents I wished I had. Shit, at one point I would have even settled for her being my sister. But my bedroom window looking into your backyard was the closest I would ever get to a perfect family. I watched you guys with Paisley. Day after day, chasing her through the sprinkler, playing tag, catch, trying to see who could pop the biggest bubble, splashing in the new pool you bought. Paisley's smiles and giggles warmed my heart. You could have never known that the little girl you waved at when you caught me watching was terrified, locked in my room and hoping my bitch mother would remember to feed me. I don't know when it became Paisley's fault, but it did. If I'm honest, I blamed you guys too, for not seeing that I needed help. I hated you. I hated Paisley. When I ran away, I knew I wouldn't get to watch you guys anymore. No more backyard barbecues, no more perfect family. So, I burned your house down. I was seventeen with anger issues, give me a break. I didn't mean for you to die, just Paisley. But she was in Georgia, visiting dear childhood friends. Lucky her, as always. When you guys died in the fire, I promised myself, I wouldn't kill Paisley. She was broken, why fix her? That all changed when she made me kill my mother. I had a chance to get the life I longed for, and she ruined it. Hey, sleeping with William was better than killing her though, right? So, don't look at me like that. But because of Willard, memories resurfaced, angry memories. Now, when I look at Paisley, I just want her dead again. I mean, at least she'll join you guys. You should be happy about that. I'll make sure she gets a spot next to you".

Serenity stands to her feet and tosses a single black rose at Paisley's mother's headstone. Another at Paisley's father's headstone, her freckled face sullen.

# Acknowledgements

While I wrote this book, I had a lot of inspiration surrounding me. I want to take a second and personally thank those who were here for me when I needed advice, guidance, motivational pushes, and so on.

My wife, Marisa, said I could only acknowledge her as Royal Highness Queen of my Children, Moon of my Stars Lol. Thank you for listening to all my crazy ideas and helping me to mold them into carefully crafted scenes. There were a lot of times where I just needed an extra ear and another mind to help me work out what I was trying to achieve, and you provided that. Many scenes came to life through your advice and on top of that, thank you for supporting my dream. Thank you for your encouragement and motivation. When there were times of doubt, you kept me going. You pushed me to write my heart out. Most of all, thank you for just being you. You are an incredible wife. Our children and I are lucky to have you. I love you.

To my mom, Kitten, thank you for encouraging me to follow my dream of becoming a writer. Thank you for taking the time to give me advice and answer my questions when I needed guidance to ensure realism in some of the scenes. Thank you for believing in me throughout this journey. Your love and support in everything I do has given me the motivation and confidence to believe in my ideas for this book.

To my dad, Tim, thank you for being a good example of hard work and dedication. In watching you with your business, I have learned that success is earned, not given. You've helped me with ideas on how to market myself and my books and I appreciate that. Thank you for supporting my dream and believing in me.

I also want to thank myself for never giving up. Through all my trials and errors, I believed I could do this. I want to thank myself for grinding through long nights and early mornings writing through bloodshot eyes. Thank you for kicking procrastinations ass and skipping movies and PS4 time so I can write. Thank you for finding my passion, sticking with it, and pouring my heart and soul into every page. Thank you for having the confidence to share my writing with the world. Thank you for stepping out of my comfort zone to follow my dream. I want to thank myself for working hard to give my family the future they deserve. I want to thank myself for writing the story I want, not the story I think the world wants. Thank you for finding time to write while not losing sight of the importance of spending quality time with my family.

And last but not least, to my readers, thank you for taking the time to read my novel and for supporting me in this journey. I truly appreciate each and every one of you. I hope you enjoyed reading it as much as I enjoyed writing it.

# About the Author: Emory

I am a proud husband and father of three. When I am not writing, I enjoy spending quality time with my family. What I like to do for fun is play basketball, watch movies with my wife, and grill or bake desserts. My baking may be the ugliest thing you've ever laid eyes on, but it tastes delicious I swear. Lol. This is also how I came up with the name of my website which is listed below. I also enjoy long walks in the park Lol just kidding, right now my wife and I only get long walks in the grocery store.

Here's how to connect with me. Follow me on Facebook at https://www.facebook.com/Author-Emory-2155222038101560/

Made in the USA
Middletown, DE
07 July 2019